T0316222

Bello:
hidden talent rediscovered!

Bello is a digital only imprint of Pan Macmillan,
established to breathe new life into previously published,
classic books.

At Bello we believe in the timeless power of the imagination,
of good story, narrative and entertainment and we want to use
digital technology to ensure that many more readers
can enjoy these books into the future.

We publish in ebook and Print on Demand formats
to bring these wonderful books to new audiences.

About Bello:

www.panmacmillan.com/imprints/bello

About the author:

www.panmacmillan.com/author/andrewgarve

Andrew Garve

Andrew Garve is the pen name of Paul Winterton (1908–2001). He was born in Leicester and educated at the Hulme Grammar School, Manchester and Purley County School, Surrey, after which he took a degree in Economics at London University. He was on the staff of *The Economist* for four years, and then worked for fourteen years for the *London News Chronicle* as reporter, leader writer and foreign correspondent. He was assigned to Moscow from 1942–5, where he was also the correspondent of the BBC's Overseas Service.

After the war he turned to full-time writing of detective and adventure novels and produced more than forty-five books. His work was serialized, televised, broadcast, filmed and translated into some twenty languages. He is noted for his varied and unusual backgrounds – which have included Russia, newspaper offices, the West Indies, ocean sailing, the Australian outback, politics, mountaineering and forestry – and for never repeating a plot.

Andrew Garve was a founder member and first joint secretary of the Crime Writers' Association.

Andrew Garve

THE
GOLDEN DEED

First published in 1960 by Collins

This edition published 2012 by Bello
an imprint of Pan Macmillan, a division of Macmillan Publishers Limited
Pan Macmillan, 20 New Wharf Road, London N1 9RR
Basingstoke and Oxford
Associated companies throughout the world

www.panmacmillan.com/imprints/bello
www.curtisbrown.co.uk

ISBN 978-1-4472-1584-4 EPUB
ISBN 978-1-4472-1583-7 POD

Visit **www.panmacmillan.com** to read more about all our books
and to buy them. You will also find features, author interviews and
news of any author events, and you can sign up for e-newsletters
so that you're always first to hear about our new releases.

Chapter One

They might have been any small family party as they made for the Somerset coast that August afternoon. In fact they were the Mellanbys. Sally Mellanby was driving the car, a new Rover. She was slim and attractive, with large brown eyes and an expressive face. The jade-green sun frock she wore set off her brown skin to perfection. Her dark hair swung loose on her shoulders. She looked about twenty-five, but in fact she was thirty-two. Beside her in the car sat six-year-old Alison, curly-haired, observant, and immensely self-possessed. In the back were eight-year-old Tony, a solid, freckled boy in T-shirt and swimming trunks, who sat clutching a partially-inflated air-bed that he intended to use as a raft – and Kira. Kira was the Norwegian girl who had come to Sally as nurse-help for the summer holidays. She was eighteen, blonde, charming, and very placid, and she fitted perfectly into the lively Mellanby household.

The moment Sally stopped the car, Alison was off with her bucket and spade, racing along the familiar dune path to 'their place' – a sheltered grass-covered hollow above the beach. Tony blew more air into his air-bed before following her. It was a very old air-bed and leaked from the nozzle, but it made a jolly good raft all the same, according to him. Sally and Kira unloaded rugs, towels and tea basket from the boot and toiled after the children.

At the top of the bank they almost collided with Alison, who was racing back full of indignation. 'Mummy,' she gasped, 'there's a man in our place – a man!'

Sally looked along the sand-bank. Above the hollow a pair of swimming trunks had been spread out to dry and an expanse of brown male chest was just visible through the marram grass. 'Well, never mind,' she said equably, 'there are plenty of other places.' Even in August, this stretch of beach was usually quiet. 'Let's go over there.' She pointed, and led the way to another little nook. Kara spread the rug and they all changed into their swim suits. Sally said she intended to sun-bathe before going into the water, so Kira took the children down to the sea.

'Keep close to the edge, Tony,' Sally called after them. She watched them down to the water, and for a little while afterwards. Kira and Alison stayed in the tiny breaking waves, splashing and laughing. Tony began to paddle his raft slowly up and down with his hands, parallel to the shore. A little way out the sea was rippled by the gentle offshore breeze, but where Tony was it was as smooth and safe as a pond.

With a sigh of contentment Sally stretched out full length on the rug, turning her face up to the sun and moving her shoulders until the sand was comfortably packed down beneath them. It was a blissfully hot day, the first for more than a week. Relaxed in the sun's warmth she thought how lucky she was to be able to take full advantage of it. Really, she had almost too many blessings to count. A devoted husband whom she loved and admired, two delightful children, a beautiful home, no money worries. Leisure enough to make the bringing up of a family wholly enjoyable; leisure to share John's quiet but deep enthusiasms . . . Soon, in fact, she might have too much leisure. Perhaps the time had come to think about another baby. They had decided that two were all they could afford to educate, but that was before John had come into his inheritance. Things were very different now, and it would be rather fun – the children would love it . . . Or, of course, she could do more public work – though she didn't really see herself as an ardent committee woman. She had always found plenty to occupy her in her own home, and John liked to know she was there. Perhaps she would give up another morning a week to the Old People's Welfare, though. She enjoyed that, and there was a direct return for effort in seeing their appreciation. She hadn't the temperament, she decided, for abstract good works . . .

She sat up as a sudden howl came from the water's edge. Alison was in trouble, and as usual wasn't slow to advertise the fact Kira was bending down, examining the little girl's foot. Presently she picked her up and started to carry her in up the beach. Sally went to meet them.

'A small piece of glass, I think,' Kira said, in her careful English.

Sally inspected Alison's toe. 'It's all right,' she said, 'it's only a little cut . . .' – though in fact it was quite deep. 'We'll wrap it up – you'll look as if you've got gout. And you can pretend to be a cross old gentleman.' She fetched the TCP from the beach bag, and a clean handkerchief, and made a bandage. Alison had stopped howling, but she started again as soon as she saw a spot of blood showing through the bandage. Sally gave her some chocolate and suggested they should start unpacking the picnic basket.

It was only after several minutes that she noticed Tony. Taking advantage of the diversion, he had paddled his raft into deep water and was yards from the shore. Sally jumped up and began to run down the beach. 'Come back, Tony,' she called, 'you're much too far out. That's very naughty!' Tony grinned and started to paddle the unwieldy craft back. It turned in a circle, but came no nearer. It was almost on the edge of the rippled water, and as the offshore wind caught it the gap grew wider. In real alarm, now, Sally splashed in and began to swim after it. She wasn't much of a swimmer, but she was better than Kira. Tony was sitting up on the raft looking a bit frightened. She shouted, 'Keep still, Tony!' though she couldn't tell whether he'd heard or not. She was swimming as hard as she could but she didn't seem to be making much headway. Anxiety, as well as exertion, took her breath away. She could hear someone calling out on the beach – Kira. She swam on, with desperate, ineffective strokes. The little waves slapped in her face. Suddenly she gulped a mouthful of water and spluttered and went under. She came up gasping and panic-stricken, thrashing her arms wildly to try and keep her head out. She'd *got* to reach the raft – but it was still yards ahead . . . Another wave slopped over her and she breathed water and choked helplessly. Fear gripped her. She was

going under again . . . It was incredible, but she was going to *drown*
. . .

At that moment a strong hand seized her, holding her up while she got her breath back. A man's voice, reassuringly calm, said, 'Don't struggle – I'll soon get you in.'

'Tony . . . !' she gasped.

'He's all right,' the man said. 'I'll come back for him in a minute . . . Just relax.'

She felt his hands close on the sides of her face, she felt herself being dragged backwards through the water as he kicked out. She lay still, with her legs together and her hands by her sides, trying to make it easier for him, trying not to think. It seemed a terribly long way back. The man was gasping too when he finally drew her into the shallows. She turned and gazed fearfully out to sea. The raft was still there but it was visibly sagging. 'It'll sink,' she cried in an agonized voice. 'It *is* sinking . . . *Tony* . . . !'

'I'll get him,' the man said again. 'Don't worry . . .' He was struggling out of the clinging flannel trousers he hadn't had time to take off. In a moment he was back in the sea, striking out with a powerful fast crawl. Sally knelt in the surf, staring after him, her face rigid with fear. Kira had joined her. They didn't speak, but kept their eyes fixed on the distant moving head. Suddenly Sally drew in her breath sharply and clutched Kira's arm as the air-bed heeled over. Tony had disappeared. Then she saw that the man was there. He'd reached Tony. She could see them both now. They were coming back – but slowly, oh so slowly. The man must be exhausted . . . But now there were other people gathered from nowhere – two young men among them, who went plunging in to help just as it seemed that the bobbing figures would never make the shore. In a few seconds Tony was brought in, scared but unharmed, and Sally was scolding him with the vehemence of enormous relief, and turning to the rescuer, the brown-chested man from 'their place', who was almost spent but who managed a fleeting wry grin all the same as he fought to get his breath back.

Chapter Two

There was a period of confusion after that as people pressed around, congratulating the rescuers and offering help and advice to Sally and asking how it had happened and tut-tutting to each other about holiday dangers – but the sensation and the interest soon died. A near-drowning, after all, was a very different matter from an actual drowning. Fifteen minutes later a casual passerby would scarcely have known that anything unusual had occurred. The two young men had slipped anonymously away to cut short the embarrassment of Sally's thanks. The little knot of spectators had dispersed. The hero-in-chief had struggled back into his wet flannels and was drinking a cup of sweet tea from the vacuum flask. Kira, pale and quiet, was handing out sandwiches to Alison and Tony, whose appetites seemed not at all impaired by the adventure. Sally, anxious that the children should have no disturbing memories of the incident, was trying to keep a firm grip on her emotions, but she felt terribly shaken and mentally almost overwhelmed by the near-tragedy. As long as she lived, she would never forget that heart-stopping moment when the raft had overturned . . .

'I simply don't know how I can ever begin to thank you,' she said to their rescuer. She had said something like it several times before, but words seemed so inadequate and her relief and gratitude were so boundless that she had to go on saying it.

'Really, it was nothing,' the man said. 'I'm glad I happened to be around, that's all.'

'You must be absolutely worn out.'

He grinned, showing strong white teeth. 'I take a lot of wearing out,' he said. It was true that he looked none the worse for his terrific exertions. He was, Sally now realized, a quite unusually large man – well over six feet, and massively built. His thick black hair was clipped short, his rather heavy jaw was dark-shadowed, and he had very vivid blue eyes. The total physical effect was one of tremendous virility. He looked about forty.

'I honestly thought those last few yards were going to be too much for you,' she said.

'Well, I rather wondered myself, to tell you the truth. There was a bit of a current . . .' His manner was easy, his accent polished. 'Still, all's well that ends well.' He put his cup down on the grass and got to his feet. 'Thanks for the tea, it was just what I needed . . . Now I guess I'll be pushing along.'

'Do please tell me your name,' Sally said.

The man hesitated, then smiled. 'If you really want to know, it's Roscoe. Frank Roscoe.'

'And I'm Sally Mellanby . . . The awful boy over there is Tony, as you know – the little girl is my daughter Alison and that's Kira, from Norway.'

Roscoe smiled again, his glance resting appreciatively on Kira for a moment. 'Always wanted to go to Norway,' he said gallantly.

'Are you on holiday here?' Sally asked.

'No, I'm on business, of a sort – hoping to find a small farm I can buy, as a matter of fact . . . I should have started looking this morning, but the weather was so good I decided to take time off and have a day on the beach.'

'Thank goodness you did . . .!' Sally was watching with some concern as Roscoe struggled to tuck his shirt into his sodden trousers. 'You're going to be terribly uncomfortable in those wet things . . . Have you far to go?'

'Not really – just a few miles.'

'You've got a car, have you?'

'No I came by bus and walked along the beach.'

'Then we must take you home. You can't possibly go on a bus like that.'

'Oh, I shall soon dry – I don't want to break up your picnic.'

'Heavens, we're not in the mood for picnics now – at least, I'm not . . . Where are you staying?'

'I don't suppose you'd know it – it's a little place called Fresney Stoke, near Bath. I'm at a pub there.'

'But we live in Bath,' Sally told him, 'we know it very well . . . We'll drop you off on the way – it couldn't be easier . . .'

'Well, it's extremely kind of you . . .'

'It's the very least we can do . . . Come on, children, get ready.'

'I'll fetch the rest of my things,' Roscoe said. He went off into the sand-hills.

In a few minutes everyone was dressed and all the belongings were gathered up. Roscoe rejoined the party and they all set off over the bank. Alison's toe, forgotten during tea, had begun to hurt again now, she declared, and Roscoe carried her, lifting her on to his shoulder as though she were a feather. Tony marched beside him, glancing up at him every few seconds in unconcealed admiration. When they reached the car Kira took the children in the back and Roscoe got in beside Sally.

'What sort of farm are you looking for, Mr Roscoe?' she asked, as they left the sandy track and turned into the high road.

'Oh – something, quite small – a few acres for a poultry farm, actually . . . I'm one of those redundant Army chaps too old at forty! Now I've got to find some way of turning my gratuity into a living.'

Sally gave him a sympathetic glance. 'It must be very hard – having to start life all over again in the middle . . . Have you always been in the Army?'

'Yes, I've been soldiering for more than twenty years . . . That's just the trouble, I don't know anything else . . . Still, I expect I can learn.'

'Do you know this part of the country?'

'Hardly at all. A friend of mine recommended it – said he'd heard the land around here was comparatively cheap. I hope he was right!'

'I should think it might be, away from Bath,' Sally said.

There was a little silence while she concentrated on a tricky bit of driving. Suddenly Tony piped up from the back, 'Mummy, could I have a new air-bed some time, do you think?'

Sally gave a little gasp, then joined in Roscoe's roar of laughter. 'I shouldn't think so for one moment,' she said firmly.

Roscoe grinned at Tony. 'Now that's what I call real bad timing,' he said.

It took them little more than half an hour to reach Fresney Stoke by the side roads that Sally knew well. As they ran into the attractive stone village, she said, 'Which is your pub, Mr Roscoe?'

'The Plough – just on the left, there. Very modest, but I'm having to watch the old shekels at the moment . . . Fine – that'll do nicely . . .'

Sally brought the car to a stop, and turned to him. 'I know my husband will be most anxious to meet you,' she said. 'If you're not doing anything, would you come and have dinner with us tomorrow evening?'

Roscoe made a deprecatory gesture. 'That's very kind of you, Mrs Mellanby – and I'd like to . . . But it really isn't necessary, you know. It was a chance encounter – could have happened to anyone.'

'You saved our lives,' Sally said gently, 'and you could very easily have lost your own. That makes the encounter rather special, don't you think?'

'All the same . . .'

'I'm certain my husband would never forgive me if he didn't have the chance to say "Thank you" himself . . . Won't you give us the pleasure of your company?'

'Well, if you put it like that I'll be very happy to come, of course . . . Where exactly do you live?'

'Don't worry about that,' Sally said. 'I'll come and fetch you . . . How would it be if I picked you up here at half past six? – that will give us plenty of time for drinks before dinner.'

'It would be fine,' Roscoe said. 'I'll look forward to it . . .' He got out of the car, still dripping a little, and pushed the door shut. Then he stuck his head in at the window. 'I say, you won't tell anyone about this, will you? About our little adventure, I mean?

I wouldn't want any of those newspaper wallahs trying to make a story out of it.'

'But it *is* a story,' Sally said. 'Everyone, ought to know about it.'

'No, no . . . If any newspapers do get in touch with you, Mrs Mellanby, please don't tell them anything. I'd hate any publicity – Army training, you know. Anyway, I'd feel such a fool . . . I mean it!'

'Well – all right,' Sally said reluctantly. 'Though I think you're much too modest.'

She smiled, and Roscoe waved to the children and gave Sally and Kira an informal salute. Then he strode away into the pub.

'I like that man,' Tony said.

Chapter Three

As he changed his clothes and spruced himself up in his small, plainly-furnished bedroom, Roscoe was aware of a pleasurable excitement – the excitement of a traveller contemplating a new journey. It was too soon yet, of course, to know just how rewarding the trip would be, or indeed whether it would be worth undertaking at all – but the preliminary indications seemed hopeful. What he needed now was more information.

As soon as opening time arrived he made his way to the saloon bar. The door was ajar, and he glanced inside before entering. The landlord of the Plough, shirt-sleeved, obese and elderly, was leaning against the counter reading a newspaper. There were no other customers yet. Roscoe went in.

'Evening!' he said cheerfully.

'Evening, sir.'

'I'll have a double whisky, please. Haig.'

The landlord nodded. 'Grand day it's been,' he said, as he turned to the bottles behind him.

'Wonderful!'

'Bit different to what we've been having.'

'I'll say.'

The whisky glass clanked on the counter. 'There you are, sir – four and six . . . Did you manage to get your swim?'

'I did indeed!' Roscoe said, with a secret smile. He put down a ten shilling note and reached for the soda. 'Would you care to join me in a drink?'

'That's very kind of you, sir – I'll have a light ale.' The landlord poured the beer and raised his glass in salute.

'Cheers!' Roscoe said, and drank. 'Well I must say it's a lovely bit of country you've got around here.'

'Very nice, isn't it?'

'Have you lived in these parts long?'

'I've been in this house thirty years.'

'Really? – then you must know the district pretty well. I wonder if you know some people named Mellanby?'

'Mellanby . . . ? Do you mean Mr John Mellanby?'

'Could be. I met a Mrs Mellanby today – dark, very attractive, with a couple of nice kids.'

'That's right, sir, that would be the Mellanbys. Everyone round here knows *them* – well, *of* them, anyway. They're pretty big shots in Bath.'

'Are they?'

'Oh, yes – they're always being written about in the papers. Public work, you know – not her so much, but he's always busy – president of this and that, helping on committees – you know the sort of thing . . .'

'Useful chap!' Roscoe said.

'Oh, they're fine people, the Mellanbys, and very well liked. Do a lot of good and don't throw their weight about too much – not like some!'

Roscoe sipped his whisky thoughtfully. This was really beginning to sound most promising – always supposing there was enough in it to make it worth while. A conscientious type, Mellanby, obviously. High-minded. Might just be the right material for Plan II . . . Roscoe continued to explore the ground.

'What does he do for a living – do you know?'

'John Mellanby? – oh, I don't think he does anything now . . . He's interested in all those bits and pieces the Romans left about – always writing about them – but that's just a hobby . . . Used to be a lecturer at Bristol, I seem to remember – but he gave that up . . . He's one of the lucky ones doesn't need to work.'

'Well off, is he?'

'Oh, he's well off, all right. Very generous he's been with his money, too – you can always count on him for a subscription if the cause is good. New hospital wing, new hall for the Youth Club, that kind of thing. He must have given thousands away ... Got it all from an uncle some little time ago – it was in the papers. I forget how much now, but it was a tidy sum. I wouldn't be surprised if he was one of the richest men in Bath.'

'Really!' Roscoe smiled, and pushed his empty glass forward. 'I think I'll have another double, landlord.'

Chapter Four

The Mellanbys' home was a long, two-storied Georgian house standing in a beautiful walled garden on the western outskirts of Bath. With its fine front doorway and lovely fanlight, its white sash windows immaculate against the rosy brick of its walls, its inner spaciousness and well-proportioned comfort, it was a house built to be lived in with pleasure and pride. Even in England's most splendid Georgian city it stood out as a work of dignity and integrity, a flawless example of the period. John Mellanby had preferred it to the exquisite Regency terraces in the centre of the town because it was so much quieter to work in. One end was given up entirely to the children; at the other end he had his study. There were no traffic noises to speak of, and he could bury himself in his writing without fear of interruption.

For a man of independent means, he worked extremely hard. At the moment he was engaged on a considerable project – a scholarly survey of the ancient monuments of Somerset, which occupied him for four or five hours a day when he wasn't out on field work or taken away from it by civic duties in the town. He liked to keep to a regular schedule, both from temperament and from earlier habit acquired at the University, where for years he'd had to earn his living like everyone else. The fortune he had inherited had neither spoiled nor embarrassed him. He was much too active a man, as well as too self-disciplined, ever to fall into idleness; and in addition to the many good causes he supported, he had found a rewarding use for Uncle Edward's capital in the financing of excavations in the county which otherwise might have had to wait for decades.

That afternoon, as the weather was so fine, he had taken his books and papers out on to the lawn and was working there in the shade of a spreading copper beech. He was a slimly-built man of medium height, with sensitive, fine-boned features, rather hollow cheeks, a long, lean chin, and a pleasantly quizzical expression about the eyes. The general effect was somewhat ascetic, but appearances – as Sally had often teasingly said – were misleading. In his quiet way, Mellanby enjoyed life deeply, and in all its aspects.

He was still absorbed in his notes when the family came back. He hadn't expected them home till after six and he looked up in surprise as the Rover turned into the drive. The two children, he noticed, were both in the back with Kira, which was unusual. After a moment he put his papers down and went over to the car. He walked with a slight limp, the result of an accident to his left leg ten years before.

One glance at Sally's face was enough to tell him that something was badly wrong. He said, in an anxious tone, 'What's happened, darling?'

'I'll tell you later,' she said. Her voice was well-controlled, but Mellanby could sense the underlying strain. 'There's nothing to worry about now.'

'Mummy and Tony were nearly drownded!' Alison said importantly.

Mellanby shot Sally a look of horror, an incredulous, questioning look, and she gave a little nod. 'Kira, would you be an angel and take the children on to the back lawn for a while?'

'Of course,' Kira said. 'Come, children.' She gathered them up and went off with them down the garden.

Sally said, 'Let's go upstairs, John, we can talk better there.'

Mellanby followed her. In their room, with the door shut Sally looked at him for a tremulous moment and then flung herself weeping into his arms. 'Oh, John, it's been so awful ... Darling, hold me tight.'

He held her, soothing and comforting her through the wild storm of tears, waiting until her shaking sobs had quietened. Then, at last, in breathless, jerky sentences, she told him what had happened.

He said, *'Sally!* – oh, my darling!' and held her closer. His face was drawn and white. He was an imaginative man. Listening to her, he knew her terror as though he had suffered it himself.

'It all happened so quickly, John . . . One minute everything was all right, and then before I even had time to think I was struggling in the water and Tony was out of reach and I was absolutely certain we were both going to be drowned. I can hardly believe it, now . . . Oh, darling, I feel so terrible about it, I know it was all my fault . . .' Tears of contrition gathered in her eyes. 'I ought to have been watching him better, but it never occurred to me for a moment he could get carried out like that, just in a few seconds . . . Poor Tony, he looked so small and helpless – and I was so cross with him afterwards.'

'Is he very upset?'

'He doesn't show any signs . . . They both know it was a narrow escape, but I don't think they really feel it. It'll be just an adventure to Tony by tomorrow . . .' Sally gave a tearful little laugh. 'It's funny – I suppose in a way it serves me right, because just before it happened I was thinking how lucky I was!'

Mellanby pressed his face against her hair. 'Well – you are!'

'Yes . . . Oh, John, it feels so *wonderful* to be home, and all of us safe . . . It would have been so ghastly for you, it makes me want to cry all over again . . . Darling, try not to blame me too much, won't you . . . ?'

'I don't blame you at all,' Mellanby said. 'I think you were very brave. You know you're a rotten swimmer.'

'Oh – that was pure instinct . . . Anyway, there was no one else about except Kira – at least, I didn't think so, I'd forgotten about the man . . . Darling, I've asked him to come and have dinner with us tomorrow, is that all right? I thought you'd want to meet him.'

'Of course,' Mellanby said. 'What did you say his name was?'

'Roscoe – Frank Roscoe.'

'What's he like?'

'Well – he's big and dark, and rather good-looking in a military sort of way, and about your age, I should think . . . He seems very nice and he's certainly very impressive. He really *did* risk his life, and he didn't hesitate at all – the way he went straight back in after he'd pulled me out was marvellous . . . He's terribly bashful about it all and I think he'd really have liked to go straight off afterwards the way those other two did, but of course I couldn't let him . . . We owe him so much.'

Mellanby nodded. Once before, when Tony was on the way and things had suddenly gone wrong, he had been faced with the prospect of life without Sally. He would never forget the creeping blankness of those hours, the near-despair. The idea, like eternity, had seemed too awful for the mind to grasp. Since then, they'd grown still closer together, in companionship and love. Sally had become so much a part of him that to lose her now seemed utterly unthinkable. Yet it had nearly happened . . .

'I owe him everything,' he said simply. 'It's rather a frightening thought . . .'

'Well, darling,' Sally said, 'we must try to do something about it. I know we can't possibly hope to repay him but there may be some practical things we can do . . . From what he said, I should think he's going to have a bit of a struggle over this farm, and he seems to be very much on his own, so perhaps we'll be able to help him in some way – if he's not too proud.'

'I certainly hope so,' Mellanby said.

Chapter Five

Roscoe was waiting on the seat outside the Plough when Sally called for him at half past six the following evening. He looked so different from the bedraggled figure she had set down there the day before that for a moment she had difficulty in recognizing him. Now he looked cool and comfortable in a well-cut light grey suit, spotless white shirt, and deerskin suède shoes. With his tanned face, his careful grooming, and his air of easy confidence, his appearance, Sally thought, was quite distinguished. She gave him a warm smile and he smiled back, running an approving eye over her.

'Well, I wouldn't say *you* were showing any signs of shock,' he said, as he got into the car beside her.

'Thank you . . . It's amazing what a good sleep will do.'

'How's Tony today?'

'Still lamenting his lost air-bed – but otherwise it might never have happened.'

'And the foot?'

'The foot? Oh – Alison. She's all right, too . . . What a memory you have!'

'It's a matter of training,' Roscoe said, with a grin.

'How is your search going? Have you started yet?'

'Well, I've not actually looked at anything, but I've put out a few feelers – got in touch with one or two agents, you know . . . Quite a hectic morning, as a matter of fact. Bath seems pretty crowded.'

Sally nodded, watching the road. 'It's the busiest time just now – right at the holiday peak.'

'What's it like in the winter? – dead, I suppose?'

'No – just quiet. We think it's very pleasant – but then we like a rather tranquil life.'

'Don't you ever get bored?'

'Bored! – good heavens, no. There are always the children, and my husband works at home a good deal.'

'What's his line?' Roscoe inquired innocently.

'Well, he's mostly an antiquarian, but he has a lot of other interests, too – various societies and committees ... People are always asking him to do things ...'

'Good works, eh? Useful citizen! Highly respected in the community.' The touch of mockery in Roseoe's tone surprised Sally.

'Well, yes, I suppose he is,' she said.

'It doesn't sound too exciting.'

'It's not exciting – but it's often very interesting.' She smiled across at him. 'If it comes to that, I don't suppose you'll find poultry farming exactly a riot!'

Roscoe grinned back at her. 'You've got a point there,' he said.

As the car turned in through the wrought-iron gates, Mellanby came out into the drive to greet his guest, his limp a little more marked than usual because of his nervousness. He was always rather shy at first encounters, and this particular encounter was a real ordeal. His massive obligation to Roscoe weighed on him. He grasped the big hand the visitor extended to him a shade longer than he would normally have done.

'I'm so glad you were able to come,' he said, and paused. 'My wife has told me all about what happened yesterday – your very brave action ... It's difficult to find words to express my gratitude for what you did. I can only say, thank you from the bottom of my heart ... I owe you more than I can ever repay.'

'Oh, there was nothing to it,' Roscoe said breezily. 'Some chaps have a way of leaping straight in in an emergency and thinking afterwards, and that's what I happen to be like. It's the way you're made – there's no credit in it. I'm glad everything turned out all right, that's all . . .' He gave a boyish smile. 'I'd really be happier if you'd forget all about it.'

'I'm not likely to do that,' Mellanby said, 'but I understand . . . Let's go and have a drink, shall we?' With a friendly pressure on Roscoe's arm he conducted him to chairs set out round a little table under the copper beech. 'We thought it might be pleasanter to sit out here, as it's so warm . . . What would you like? Gin and something? Sherry . . .?'

'Gin and French for me, if that's all right,' Roscoe said. He gazed around as Mellanby busied himself with ice and glasses, taking in the gracious house, the well-tended garden, the two smart cars parked one behind the other in the drive . . .

'Nice place you've got here,' be said with enthusiasm. 'Beautiful house!'

'It's very attractive, isn't it?' Mellanby agreed. 'A design they're never likely to improve on . . .'

'I bet it's nice inside, too . . . Lots of genuine Chippendale?'

Mellanby smiled. 'Well, no – but there are some nice things – some lovely Adam fireplaces, for instance, if you're interested. Perhaps you'd like to look round later on?'

'I would indeed . . .' Roscoe turned to Sally. 'Don't you find servants are a problem for a place like this, Mrs Mellanby?'

'We haven't had much difficulty so far,' Sally said. 'Cook and our daily maid both live fairly near, so they can go home at night, and I think that keeps them happy . . .'

Roscoe gave a little nod. Mellanby finished mixing the drinks and handed them round.

'Well, this is quite an occasion,' he said, raising his glass. 'Your very good health, Roscoe!'

'Happy days!' Roscoe said.

They drank. Sally took one of the chairs and the men followed her example. Mellanby passed the cigarettes to Roscoe, and lit his pipe. He was beginning to look more at ease.

'Well,' he said, 'my wife tells me you've just left the Army.'

'Yes . . . I was a major in the Gloucester when they bowler-hatted me.'

'And now you're planning to become a chicken farmer?'

'That's the general idea. I may be crazy – but I've always been used to an open-air life and I know I'd never be able to stand a desk job. Ordinary farming's more than I could tackle, but I think I could manage poultry – and some people seem to make a living at it.'

'I expect you've been pretty thoroughly into the economics of it,' Mellanby said.

'Oh, yes, I think I know the form. I've been browsing in the books quite a lot – you can pick up a good bit there . . .' Roscoe grinned. 'At least I can tell the difference between a White Leghorn and a Rhode Island Red now.'

'It's more than I can,' Mellanby said. He puffed thoughtfully at his pipe for a moment. 'You know, I should think it might help if you could talk to someone who's actually running a poultry farm. I can't think of anyone offhand, but I'm sure we could find someone . . .'

'That would be a great help,' Roscoe agreed. 'One of my troubles is that I don't know a soul in this country, apart from a few chaps who came out of the Army at the same time – and I've even lost sight of them, now . . . I've been abroad so long I feel almost like a stranger here – I don't even know where my relations are, supposing I've still got any . . . But I expect I'll soon make some friends.'

'You've made some,' Sally said, with a smile.

'Well – that's jolly nice of you.'

'What you really need, of course,' Sally said, 'is a wife. Are you married?'

'No – somehow I never seemed to get around to it. But I probably will take a wife when I'm a bit more settled – must have someone to collect the eggs! First I've got to find a place, though.'

'What sort of thing have you in mind?' Mellanby asked him.

'Oh, something quite small – the old gratuity won't run to anything ambitious. About three acres, I thought.'

'As little as that?'

'Well, I'll be working on the battery system, you know – keeping the jolly old birds inside, with nothing to do but lay. You don't need a lot of ground for that. On three acres I reckon I can have six or seven hundred birds – and that's as many as I can handle on my own. Even for that number the capital outlay will be pretty steep.'

'What about a house?' Mellanby asked.

'Oh, almost anything will do for me, to start with. It'll have to be something very simple – a shack, or a small bungalow, perhaps.'

Sally said, 'You know, John, Eleanor's been talking vaguely about selling *her* cottage and field – it might be the very thing if she could be brought to part with it . . .' She explained to Roscoe. 'Eleanor Bryce is a friend of mine – we work together on the Old People's Welfare here. She lives at Marples – that's about seven miles away . . . It's a charming little cottage, not modernized but full of possibilities. Would you like me to ask her about it?'

'That's very decent of you,' Roscoe said. 'It sounds as though it might be a bit grand for me, but the more places I can inspect, the sooner I'll get my ideas sorted out.'

Mellanby, looking thoughtful, got up to refill the glasses. 'It's certainly going to be quite an undertaking,' he said, 'starting from scratch the way you're doing.'

Roscoe nodded. 'It'll be all right if the money holds out.'

Mellanby said, 'Yes,' and frowned. He was a fastidious man, and there was something very distasteful about offering financial help as a direct return for the saving of lives. Roscoe might easily feel the same way about it. Yet the subject had been raised – and now was surely the time to show willingness. As casually as he could, he said, 'Well, if an interest-free loan would help you over the hump in the early stages, you've only to tell me.'

'That's most generous of you,' Roscoe said gratefully. 'I'll certainly bear it in mind . . . But I'd like to stand on my own feet as far as possible.'

'Talking of standing on your own feet,' Mellanby said, with a faint smile, 'how are you planning to get about while you're looking for a place? Sally tells me you haven't a car.'

'No, I haven't . . . I managed to get myself through the driving test the other day, so I've got a licence, but the car will have to wait till I can see my way more clearly . . .' He grinned. 'Got the snaffle and the bit but no jolly old horse, eh? I guess I'll have to rely on public transport.'

Mellanby shook his head. 'I'd have thought a car would be absolutely essential while you're searching. You're bound to be covering a lot of ground, and you'll find public transport very thin as soon as you get off the main roads . . . Look, why not borrow my car?'

'Ah, no – it's very good of you, Mellanby, but you'll be needing it yourself.'

'We've got two cars, as you can see. I can easily share Sally's.'

Roscoe looked doubtfully at Sally. 'What about all those old people you visit, Mrs Mellanby? – that must mean a lot of running about for you. I'm sure it would be most inconvenient.'

'I don't do very much in the holidays,' Sally said. 'I like to be with the children when they're at home . . . Really, we shan't be needing both cars – there's no reason at all why you shouldn't have one.'

'H'm – well, it's darned nice of you, I must say, and very tempting . . . It would make a lot of difference – save me hours of footslogging . . . Are you sure about it, Mellanby?'

'You'll be more than welcome,' Mellanby said. 'Take the Humber with you tonight.'

'Well,' Roscoe said, with obvious relief, 'if I can really do that it'll ease another problem for me . . . It looks as though the first thing I'll have to do in the morning is find new lodgings.'

'Oh?'

'Yes, the Plough's booked up solid after tonight, so I've got to shift, I tried a couple of other places in the village, but they're full, too, and they tell me Bath's chock-a-block . . . Still, I expect I'll find something . . .'

Mellanby and Sally exchanged glances. There was a little pause. Then Sally said, 'Won't you come and stay with us, Mr Roscoe? We'd be so pleased if you would, and we've lots of room.'

Roscoe looked quite taken aback. 'Oh, no – I couldn't do that

– it would be an imposition. You people are much too kind . . . After all, I'm just a stranger . . .'

'We don't feel you're a stranger,' Sally said, 'and we'd be delighted to have you . . . In fact, we insist, darling, don't we?'

'We do indeed,' Mellanby said. One of us will collect you at the Plough tomorrow morning, Roscoe, and you can use this house as a base until you're fixed up. All right?'

'I'm overwhelmed,' Roscoe said. 'But I can't pretend it wouldn't make things a darned sight easier for me – and apart from that, I'd enjoy it a lot.'

'Then it's settled,' Sally said. She stood up as she caught sight of Mrs Barney, the cook, at the open front door. 'After dinner I'll show you your room.'

Chapter Six

Roscoe moved in on the following morning, with one large suitcase, a stack of poultry journals, and a few oddments. The rest of his belongings, he explained, were being stored in London until he had somewhere to put them. Mellanby said he was welcome to have them sent down right away, but Roscoe said he'd got used to living out of a suitcase and could manage perfectly well. Sally told him he must regard himself as one of the family and make himself absolutely at home, and he said he would. By lunchtime he was 'Frank' to Kira and 'Uncle Frank' to the children.

Sally had already rung up Eleanor Bryce to find out if her cottage and field were really for sale, and it seemed that they were. The cottage was standing empty, Eleanor had said, and the key was at the farmhouse next door, so Mr Roscoe could inspect it any time he wished. Roscoe said there was no time like the present and went of immediately after lunch in Mellanby's Humber. He drove out of the gate and down the normally sedate road a great deal faster than the Mellanbys ever did, but he had assured Sally he was a very safe driver – 'it's the slow ones that get into trouble, you know' – and he certainly gave an impression of competence, if not of caution.

He was back about six, with a mixed report Mrs Bryce's field was a possibility, he said, though it had a northern slope, which wasn't supposed to be too good for poultry – and the cottage was a bit on the large side. It would be better, he thought, not to rush into anything before he'd had a good look round. Thanks to the car, he'd been able to inspect a couple of other properties deep in the Somerset by-ways, and he had more plans for the next day.

He seemed very hopeful about his prospects, and generally in high spirits.

The evening passed agreeably. After he'd changed, Roscoe joined Mellanby, who was having a game of cricket with the children on the back lawn. It turned out he could bowl rather cunning off-breaks, which delighted Tony. Then there were drinks outside again, and a pleasant dinner during which Roscoe amusingly described his experiences with estate agents the previous day. He was an exuberant addition to the family and a complete contrast to the gentle, urbane Mellanby. Kira, sitting opposite him, seemed quite fascinated by his male vigour and his brilliant blue eyes. As the meal progressed, the Mellanbys learned a little more about his background. His father, it seemed, had been a marine engineer at Southampton, but Roscoe had never really known him – both his parents had died when he was young. He'd been brought up by a spiritualist maiden aunt, long departed, who had held seances at her home in Beckenham – one of which, as a small boy, Roscoe had contrived to watch from a cupboard and now described with gusto. His flow of talk was most entertaining – but at ten, as though sensing that Sally and Mellanby would be glad of a quiet hour together, he said he thought he'd have an early night and went off to bed with *The Smallholder*. He was going to be, Sally decided, a model guest.

In the morning Sally rang up some of her country friends to see if they knew of a successful poultry farmer in the district. She was soon put on to a young man named Tom Adams, who turned out to be very affable and told her on the phone that he'd be glad to talk to Roscoe and give him any advice he could. Roscoe, well pleased, went straight off to see him, and was away all day.

Sally was sitting with the children under the copper beech when he drove in in the evening, scattering the gravel as he jammed the brakes on hard. This time he was bearing gifts – a huge bunch of red and white carnations. He crossed the lawn to her and presented them with a bow and a flourish. 'For you, Sally,' he said.

The familiar use of her name startled her. She said, 'That's not the way to take care of your shekels!' a trifle reprovingly. 'But they're lovely – thank you very much. Aren't they lovely, Tony?'

'Yes,' Tony said, without enthusiasm. 'Can I have the elastic?'

'I've got something better than elastic for you, young fellow-me-lad,' Roscoe told him. 'Come and see . . .' He turned back towards the drive.

Sally called after him, 'How did you get on with Mr Adams?'

'Oh, fine, fine . . . I think I've just about got the practical side sewn up, now . . .' He was already delving in the back of the car. After a moment he produced a pair of small-size boxing gloves, on which Tony fell with glee. 'Ever done any boxing at school, Tony?'

'Yes, I have, and I'm a very good boxer, except that I keep my eyes shut,' Tony said.

Roscoe gave a loud guffaw. 'Well, that's not much use, is it? – you'll have to practise . . . I'll soon teach you.' He produced another pair of gloves, for himself. Then he went round to the boot and hauled out a punchball on an adjustable stand. 'Got to keep fit!' he called to Sally, with a grin. 'Shall we take it round the back, Tony?'

Tony tried to lift the stand, but the base was of solid iron and he couldn't move it. Roscoe laughed, and threw it lightly over his shoulder. 'Come on,' he said.

Alison shed a tear or two after they'd gone. 'He didn't bring me a present,' she sobbed.

'Never mind, pet,' Sally said. 'Come and help me arrange these flowers, and then we'll turn out all the cupboards and see what we can find for the Jumble Sale.'

Alison brightened at once. 'Oh, yes!' she said. 'That'll keep me amused for a long time, won't it?'

A boxing lesson was in full swing on the back lawn when Mellanby emerged from his study at half past six. Roscoe, his magnificent torso bared to the waist, was showing Tony how to punch, while Kira stood by and watched. His tremendous blows cracked against the punchball like gunshots in the still garden. With his great rippling muscles and his agile tread he made a most impressive figure.

'Are you a heavyweight?' Tony asked, as Roscoe finally allowed the punchball to come to rest.

Roscoe nodded, with a wink at Mellanby.

'Are you a champ, too?'

'Well, I used to box for the regiment,' Roscoe said, 'and I generally managed to win ... Now you have a go.'

Tony began to batter at the punchball. Roscoe stood back, watching him. 'Good thing for young chaps to be able to use their fists,' he said to Mellanby.

Mellanby smiled and said nothing.

'Too many young sissies about, if you ask me.'

'Would you say so ...? What's your definition of a sissy?'

'Any chap who can't defend himself properly ... Pity you can't have a crack with us, Mellanby – but I guess that leg of yours would let you down.'

'I dare say the leg would be all right,' Mellanby said dryly, 'but boxing's not really my line of country.'

'How did you get the limp?' Roscoe asked. 'Trouble with the old Hun?'

'Nothing so heroic, I'm afraid. I was excavating a wall about ten years ago and slipped, and the knee's played me up ever since.'

'Bad luck, old man ... Well, come on, Tony, see if you can batter me into unconsciousness with that straight left of yours ... !'

Dinner that evening was far from the pleasant meal it had been the day before. Following his demonstration of prowess in the garden, something extraordinary seemed to have happened to Roscoe. He now appeared determined to dominate the table too, both with his physical presence and his loud talk. His way of speech, with its curious blending of BBC accent, Army slang, and transatlantic idiom, suddenly began to jar. The uninhibited cross-glances he kept throwing at Kira made Sally feel decidedly uneasy. One way and another, she scarcely recognized the well-mannered and considerate guest of the first day. Mellanby, normally so tolerant, relapsed after a while into near-silence as Roscoe continued to hold the stage. He was talking about his campaign experiences in the Western Desert; of Wogs and Wops and how he had dealt with them, and of various actions in which he had creditably taken part. He had probably drunk, Mellanby decided, just one Martini too many – the large one he had helped himself to just before dinner. It was all a bit trying. Mellanby particularly didn't like the way he kept saying 'Sally.' It was a name he cherished, a name to be use with affection by friends. A small thing, no doubt, but irritating . . .

It was Sally, when at last she was alone with Mellanby, who put their joint concern into words.

'John,' she said, 'do you think you're going to like Roscoe?'

He gave a wry smile. 'I'm having a damn good try.'

'It was awful tonight, wasn't it . . .? I simply can't imagine what got into him.'

'Gin!' Mellanby said.

'Well, yes, but I don't think it could have been only that . . . He seemed completely different today – almost like a different person . . . I don't understand him at all.'

'Neither do I,' Mellanby said, 'but then we don't really know him very well yet. We'll have to wait a bit.'

'He's a shocking exhibitionist – all that display of muscle on the lawn . . .! *I* think he was doing it to impress Kira . . .'

'Well, if you're one of those very brawny chaps I suppose it's natural to show off sometimes . . . And don't forget we were glad enough of his brawn a couple of days ago.'

'I know . . .' Sally looked distressed. 'It's dreadful that we should be talking like this about him – it seems so horribly ungrateful after what he did . . . I know I *ought* to like him – but actually I think I'm a bit afraid of him.'

'Oh, nonsense!'

'It's true . . . If he can be so arrogant after two days, what's he going to be like in a week or two? He's beginning to take possession of the house . . .'

'Really, Sally, I think you're imagining things.'

'Well, he certainly did tonight. Perhaps he'll be different tomorrow – I hope so ... I do *want* to like him – I feel quite terrible about it ... John, surely it should be easy to like someone who's saved the life of one's child?'

'I doubt if it's as simple as that' Mellanby said. 'After all, it's not a natural relationship, being so obliged to anyone. It's a forced one. I dare say there's an unconscious resentment set up.'

'I suppose there might be – but I don't think it's true in my case. I liked him very much yesterday ... And I do enormously admire him for what he did.'

'So do I,' Mellanby said, 'but admiration's not the same thing as liking. A man doesn't necessarily turn out to be compatible with oneself, simply because he's been physically brave, it's a great quality, and I wish I had it, but there are other qualities, too ... Anyhow, I shouldn't worry about it, Sally – just let things take their course ... We'll do everything we possibly can for Roscoe – and if we find he's not our sort, well, it just can't be helped ...'

Mellanby was away all next day. An Antiquaries' Summer School was being held at Weston-super-Mare, and he'd been asked to preside at the opening session. Sally usually went with him on these occasions, but this time she'd decided not to.

It was nearly ten when he got home. The house was quiet, the children were asleep. Sally was sitting alone in the garden room, with the french doors open to the warm night.

'Hallo, darling,' she said, 'I'm so glad you're back ... How did it go?'

'Oh, quite well. There were more people than last year, and a lot of them young.'

'Good speakers?'

'Jones was fascinating about the Shetland "dig." Dickson was a bit drear ...' Mellanby smiled. 'One of those lectures that seem to last a fortnight but actually only last about ten days.'

'You must be tired. Come and sit down.'

Mellanby joined her on the settee and began to fill his pipe. 'How's our friend been?'

'He was quite all right at dinner . . . At the moment, he's walking round the garden with Kira.'

Mellanby said, 'Oh!'

'I hope he's not going to turn out to be a wolf.'

'Well – Kira's not likely to come to much harm in the garden, I shouldn't think.'

'It's not just that – it's everything. Haven't you noticed how he looks at her?'

'Very much the way he looks at *you*, I'd say.'

'That's what I mean.'

'Well, you're both quite an eyeful!'

Sally smiled. 'John, do be serious for a moment – I'm really very worried. Kira's only eighteen and she's rather impressionable, and everyone knows that a foreigner often seems very attractive . . . It would be awful if she fell for him – I think we'd just have to bundle her off home. It's a bit of a responsibility . . . It isn't as though he's a young man . . . Don't you think perhaps we ought to do something about it?'

'Do you mean you'd like me to speak to him?'

'Well, I think that would be the best way . . . I *could* talk to Kira, but I don't want to upset her . . . I would feel much happier, darling, really. They're together so much here – I hate the feeling I've got to keep an eye on them. Anyways it's not possible . . . They've been out there nearly half an hour . . .' Abruptly, she got up and went to the door.

'What are you going to do?' Mellanby asked.

'I'm going to put the garden light on,' Sally said. 'It'll help them to find their way back.'

When Roscoe went out to the car in the morning, Mellanby strolled with him. It was a distasteful task he had to perform, and he was anxious to get it over.

'Have you a big programme today?' he asked.

'Four places,' Roscoe said. 'One of them sounds quite promising.'

'Good – let's hope it turns out a winner . . . By the way, Roscoe, a word in your ear. I'm sure you'll understand . . . Don't let young Kira get too fond of you.'

Roscoe swung round, gazing down at Mellanby with a truculence that was something new. 'What's the idea?'

'I gather you were walking round the garden with her last night Well, there's no harm in that, of course, not just once, but she obviously admires you, and we don't want any bother with her. She's very young, you know.'

Roscoe shrugged. 'A man in my position has to take his fun where he can get it.'

Mellanby stared at him for a moment, speechless. Then he said, 'Well, don't try to take it here, that's all.'

Roscoe looked sullen. 'I don't see . . .' he began. Then a grin spread slowly over his face. 'Okay, old man – I certainly don't want to abuse your hospitality. I'll lay off her – she's not the only well-shaped pebble on the beach. No more walks in the garden I promise.'

'Thank you,' Mellanby said coldly.

Chapter Seven

There was more trouble over Roscoe that afternoon – this time of a sort that Sally had been half-expecting all along. Around five o'clock, just as she was settling down to an instalment of Winnie the Pooh with Alison, he rang up to say he'd got in a bit of a jam with the car.

'Nothing serious,' he said, 'no casualties, and no damage to speak of – but I'm stuck and I'll need some help to get clear.'

'What's happened?' Sally asked.

'Got my near-side wing jammed against a stone wall – I was trying to pass a caravan in a lane, and there wasn't room. We're both stuck . . . What's the best place to ring for a breakdown van?'

'Where are you?'

'Well, I'm telephoning from the main road where the lane turns off. The signpost says "Eversleigh 1/2 one way and – just a minute! – "Crouch 4" the other. The lane goes to Pointings . . .'

'Oh I know the place,' Sally said, 'it's Blackett's Lane . . .'

'There's a bridge being rebuilt a little way along – looks as though they're widening it.'

'That's right . . . How far along is the car?'

'Just beyond the bridge.'

'Aren't there any workmen who can help?'

'Not a damn one, or I wouldn't have bothered you.'

'Well, I'd better ring our own garage and get them to send someone. They're very reliable.'

'Thanks a lot, Sally. Sorry to be such a nuisance – bad show, I'm afraid.'

'That's all right,' Sally said, 'it could happen to anyone . . . Don't worry.'

She rang off and dialled the garage. The owner, a phlegmatic man named Jack Reed, said the breakdown van was out on a job, but as soon as it came, in he'd take it straight round to Blackett's Lane himself. He couldn't say exactly when it would be.

Sally called Kira and asked her to take over the reading session and then went along to the study to tell Mellanby the news. He didn't seem at all surprised.

'Perhaps I ought to run over there, John,' Sally said. 'Roscoe will wonder what's happened if no one turns up.'

Mellanby pushed his papers aside. 'I'll come with you,' he said. 'We may be able to lend a hand.'

There was a real tangle in Blackett's Lane. The caravan, a large and opulent-looking cream trailer, was immovably wedged between one of the stone walls and the Humber car. The Humber was firmly locked against the other wall, with its near-side wing sprung over a pointed lump of granite. Mellanby and Sally had to go through a field gate and back over the wall to get round to the front of the obstruction. Roscoe was standing there in the road, smoking a cigarette. A few yards away a man and a woman were leaning against an unhitched black Chrysler. The glum expression on all three faces suggested that there'd been a certain amount of recrimination about the incident.

'Well – hallo!' Roscoe said in surprise, as he caught sight of the Mellanbys.

'The breakdown van won't be here yet,' Sally explained, 'so we thought we'd better come.'

Roscoe said, 'Oh!' He looked at Mellanby in some embarrassment. 'Sorry to bring *you* out, old man . . . Sorry about it all! 'Fraid I've put up a bit of a black.'

The caravan owner approached. He was a big, burly, greying man of fifty-five or so, with a florid, fleshy face and a bit of a paunch. He was wearing a plaid shirt with the sleeves rolled up, and khaki drill trousers belted over his stomach. 'It's your car, is it?' he said to Mellanby.

Mellanby nodded.

'Well, if you don't mind me saying so, this young fellow's not fit to drive it. He was going a heck of a lot too fast.'

'I'd have been all right if it hadn't been for the bridge,' Roscoe said. 'All that clutter they've left around ...! What do they want to widen a bridge, in a lane like this for, anyway?'

'They're going to widen the whole lane,' Mellanby told him, 'and bring the main road through it to by-pass Eversleigh village. It's an accident black spot.'

'So will this be if people try to bring caravans through it,' Roscoe said.

'We wouldn't have thought of it,' the caravan's owner's wife said, 'but someone told us there was an old quarry along here that would make a good stopping place. We didn't realize the lane would be quite so narrow ...' She was at least twenty years younger than the man, and very attractive – a striking brunette, with dark eyes and a beautifully curved mouth and one of the loveliest complexions Sally had ever seen.

'I know the quarry,' Sally said, with a friendly smile. 'It *would* make a nice stopping place.'

'Anyhow,' Mellanby said, 'there doesn't seem to be much harm done ...' He walked over to the wall and took a closer look at the Humber wing. 'I suppose the three of us couldn't lift it off ...?'

'We've tried it already,' Roscoe said – adding, with a slight grin, 'I doubt if you'd make much difference, old man.'

Oh, well, the breakdown crane should be able to lift it from the other side of the wall – and when it's free we can back out.'

'That's about it,' Roscoe agreed. 'Let's hope no one else tries to use the lane, that's all. . . . How long do you think it'll be before the breakdown van comes?'

'I should think it might be an hour,' Sally said.

For a moment or two they continued to stand and gaze at the road block. Then the caravan owner said, 'Well, we're not going to shift it by just looking at it. What about you folks joining my wife and me in a glass of sherry while we're waiting?'

'That's a cheerful suggestion,' Sally said.

'I reckon it's better than arguing about who's to blame . . . Come on in and see the homestead – that is, if we can get in . . . Our name's Sherston, by the way, George and Eve Sherston.' He had a bluff, direct, manner that Sally found engaging.

Sally said, 'Ours is Mellanby. This is Frank Roscoe – he's staying with us.'

Sherston nodded. 'Glad to know you all . . .' His accent and way of speech had a transatlantic flavour, but Mellanby didn't think he was American. 'Shall I go ahead . . .?'

The door of the caravan was just clear of the Humber and with a little difficulty Sherston managed to open it wide enough for them all to squeeze through.

'But what a marvellous caravan!' Sally exclaimed, gazing around at the exquisitely appointed interior.

'It is nice, isn't it?' Eve Sherston said.

'It's so roomy – why, it's more like a flat.'

'Yes – we've got a sitting-room, bedroom, kitchen and bath. It's much easier to keep clean than a flat too.'

'I love the big windows,' Sally said.

Eve nodded. 'It's almost like living out of doors, but without discomfort . . . Do come and have a look round.'

Sally followed her into the kitchen. It was a housewife's dream in miniature, with every variety of space-saving contrivance and gadget.

'I never realized caravans could be as exciting as this,' Sally said. 'How the children would love it!'

'How many children have you?' Eve asked.

'Two – a boy and a girl. Eight and six.'

'Aren't you lucky?' Eve looked very wistful. 'I adore children, but that's as far as I seem to get . . . Still, I haven't given up hope.'

Sherston was drawing the cork from a bottle of Bristol Cream as they returned to the sitting-room. 'So you like our little home, Mrs Mellanby?' he said.

'It's wonderful . . . It must be enormous fun.'

'*We* think so – which is just as well, as it's all we've got for the time being. We debated whether to stay in hotels or buy a van, and decided the van would be more free-and-easy . . .' He poured five glasses of sherry and handed them round.

'Well, this is very hospitable of you,' Mellanby said. He savoured the sherry, which was excellent. 'You're on holiday, are you?'

'That's right,' Sherston said. 'And a good long holiday it's going to be, isn't it, Eve?' His glance rested on his wife for a moment with possessive affection. 'First England, then all round Europe with a bit of luck. If it takes us years, so much the better.'

'Where are you from?' Roscoe asked.

'We're from Trinidad – British West Indies. I'm an oil man – at least, I was. Mining engineer.'

'Really?' Roscoe looked interested. 'bloke in my regiment was going out to Trinidad – chap named Curthoys. Redundant, like me. He had some notion of buying a share in a sugar estate.'

'I reckon he could do a lot worse,' Sherston said. 'They're doing well with sugar just now, and the life's very pleasant for a man who doesn't mind hard work. You've got to be pretty tough, of course – but that goes for all those places.'

'Are you planning to go back there eventually?' Sally asked.

'Well, we haven't really got around to deciding that Mrs Mellanby. The fact is, we had a big stroke of luck and we're going to enjoy ourselves – aren't we, Eve? I'm a very fortunate man. I bought myself a small Crown concession in the bush with the idea there might be oil there – and it turned out there was. So now we're sitting pretty.'

'That was very smart of you,' Roscoe said.

'Well, it's my line, of course I knew what I was doing up to a point – but there was another fellow after it so I had to act fast. I thought shall I or shan't I, and Eve said yes, and I thought yes, so I closed the deal. I reckon that's the best way to make decisions – quickly. More people regret doing nothing than doing something, in the end – don't you think so, Mr Mellanby? Impulse, that's the thing!'

Mellanby laughed. 'It certainly makes for an exciting life.'

'Sure it does! Like the way we packed up and came over here . . . Now some people would have salted away the cash for their old age and died before they reached it. Not us, though. Eve and I packed up and let the bungalow and got a boat right away. We've always done that. Act first and think afterwards. Sounds silly, doesn't it, but it works. We even got married only two days after we met – didn't we, darling? – and we've certainly never regretted the speed of that.' He looked fondly at his wife, who gave him a rather inscrutable smile and held her glass out to be refilled.

Mellanby said, 'How long are you thinking of staying around here?'

'Well, it depends what there is to see – our time's our own. We've got a lot of ground to cover, but I've heard Bath's a pretty interesting place.'

'It's unique,' Mellanby said.

'Yes, that's what they tell us . . . What would you advise us to go for?'

'Well, you'll want to see the Roman bath, of course there's nothing quite so marvellous in the whole country, to my mind. It's very much as it was two thousand years ago – you can see the worn stones where the Romans used to stand at the edge of the water, and the places they used for drying and dressing. You can see their lead pipes, and the hollow tiles they used, and a dismounting block for the chariots – it's all there, a complete bit of history.'

'That sounds tremendous,' Sherston said. 'We mustn't miss that, Eve.'

'And if you happen to be interested in architecture,' Mellanby went on, 'Bath's sheer delight, of course. Queen's Square, the Circus, the Royal Crescent – they're all perfect eighteenth century.'

'And Pulteney Bridge,' Sally put in enthusiastically.

'Yes – that's the little bridge that has houses built into it. It was designed by Robert Adam. Oh, there are no end of fascinating bits if you've got time. That boot and shoe shop near the Abbey, Sally, with the lovely bow windows . . .'

'And the house in River Street with the link extinguisher,' she said. 'It's a metal thing like a dunce's cap,' she explained to the Sherstons. 'The linkmen used to escort the sedan chairs of the well-to-do people with torches at night because the streets weren't lit, and the dunce's cap was where they put their torches out. Most of the big houses had them.'

Sherston was listening as eagerly as a schoolboy. 'Now isn't that interesting, Eve?' he said. 'I reckon we're going to be here for some time . . . And what about those famous waters they talk about so much – do you think they could get this turn of mine down, eh?' He patted his comfortable waistline.

Eve said, with a smile, 'Someone told George that a spa course was just the thing to tone one up in middle age. Do you think it works?'

'Well, I've never tried it myself,' Mellanby said, 'but a lot of people do, of course.'

'Does he *need* toning up?' Roscoe asked. He was looking at Eve Sherston – looking in such a blatantly intimate way that his meaning couldn't be mistaken. Combined with the remark, the glance was almost an indecent assault

There was an awkward silence. Sherston was gazing at Roscoe in amazement. Eve looked most uncomfortable. Mellanby felt too ashamed and embarrassed to speak. Really, the man was quite intolerable where women were concerned – an unrestrained oaf . . .!

At that moment, fortunately, there was a hoot from the lane. Roscoe said, 'That'll be the breakdown van,' and eased himself out of the door. The others followed. Jack Reed, with the two men he'd brought with him, was already sizing up the job. He nodded to Sally and Mellanby, said 'Bit of trouble, eh?' and got straight down to work.

The disentangling took quite a time. Even when the car wing was lifted it still had to be got away from the wall. But at last it was freed, and one of the garage men backed the car out, not without a few more scrapes and dents.

'You'll have to let me know what the bill is, Mr Mellanby,' Sherston said. 'I'll be happy to pay half.'

'Oh, it won't amount to much,' Mellanby said. 'You needn't worry about that.'

'Well, it *was* partly our fault – this lane sure is narrow . . . How much further do we have to go before we reach the quarry?'

'Only a couple of hundred yards or so.'

'Oh – then I guess we should make it without difficulty . . . Well, I must say it's been fine meeting you people . . .' Sherston's cordial glance embraced Mellanby and Sally, but ostentatiously excluded Roscoe.

Eve smiled at Sally. 'I wonder if you'd care to bring the children along to see the caravan some time, Mrs Mellanby? It would be so nice if you would.'

'Do you mean it?' Sally said. 'I know they'd adore it.'

'Of course I mean it. Come and have tea one afternoon. I don't know what George's plans are, exactly – perhaps the best thing would be for me to give you a ring.'

Sally nodded. 'The number's Bath 41004 . . . It's in the book.'

'Lovely,' Eve said. 'I shall look forward to it.'

Chapter Eight

Sally and Mellanby had two more days to study Roscoe's peculiar personality before the next major incident occurred. During that time, his behaviour was so unpleasant that they could no longer have any doubts about their feeling towards him.

There was something, they decided, almost unbalanced about the way he made trouble. He did it quite unnecessarily and irresponsibly, loosing malicious verbal shafts out of the blue with no provocation whatever, just as he'd done at the caravan. His chief target was the patient Mellanby, to whom he was insolent and patronizing by turns. But the others didn't escape. The children came in for a good deal of mischievous teasing – not without protests from Sally – and were several times reduced to tears. Kira, perhaps, suffered most of all. Roscoe had not been content merely to carry out his promise and keep his attentions within bounds – now he had gone to the other extreme and was treating her like a menial, sending her off to post letters and buy cigarettes for him as though she were his personal servant. To the Mellanbys his behaviour was quite unaccountable – it was as though, in some desperately perverse way, he was driven to make people dislike him, to turn friends into enemies, to destroy. True, he was unpredictable – he could still, if he happened to be in the mood, switch on the charm and be the unexceptionable guest. But the total impact of his Jekyll-and-Hyde character upon the household was calamitous. What had been an exceptionally harmonious and tranquil home was rapidly turning into a moody and irritable one.

Only Mellanby's profound sense of obligation prevented him from asking his guest to leave at once. He discussed it all with

Sally in a long, anxious session and they agreed that if things got no better the moment was bound to come – and probably very soon. But Mellanby was deeply reluctant to take the step before he had to. The recollection of what he had so nearly lost, of the immense debt he owed to this strange, schizophrenic man, was so fresh in his mind that he shrank from the ingratitude of an ultimatum. Considering what Roscoe had done for them, he said, it was really a very minor sacrifice they were making – and they'd feel much happier in the end if his departure came naturally. It wasn't as though he were showing any signs of settling in – he was still busily combing the district for his farm and with a bit of luck they wouldn't have to put up with him much longer ... Sally, torn by the same inward conflict as Mellanby, agreed ...

Then, five days after Roscoe's arrival at the house, there was a most disconcerting episode. It happened before dinner, when Sally and Mellanby were in the garden. The telephone rang, and Kira answered it in the sitting-room. The call was for Roscoe, who had just returned from a long day in the country. He came quickly downstairs to take it. Mellanby hoped it might have something to do with clinching a property deal, but evidently it hadn't. The caller, whoever he was, was extremely angry. Harsh crackling sounds were audible through the open window as far away as the copper beech. Roscoe, holding the receiver away from his ear, glanced a little sheepishly across the lawn.

Snatches of one-sided conversation followed, on a rising pitch of temper never before heard in the Mellanby house. 'I don't see you've anything to make a fuss about, old chap ...' – 'Don't be so bloody silly, it was only a friendly gesture ...' – and, more aggressively, '*You'd* better watch your step, too, or you'll get hurt – I'm not used to being threatened ...' Presently, with another glance across the lawn, Roscoe reached out and closed the window and the Mellanbys heard no more.

Roscoe didn't come out for his usual drink when the conversation was over. He went straight back upstairs, with an ugly scowl on his face – and stayed there.

Mellanby said quietly, 'I wonder what mischief he's been up to now!'

'I don't know, he sounded horrible . . .' Sally looked tense. 'Darling, I don't think I can stand much more of him – really.'

'Not if he's going to be like that, I agree.'

'I think we ought to set a limit for ourselves,' Sally said. 'I think we should give him just two more days and then ask him, in as friendly a way as we can, to find somewhere else to stay . . . I don't a bit mind him going on using the car, or you helping him, or anything – I just don't want to have him in the house.'

Mellanby looked at her in silence for a moment. Then he said, 'All right, Sally . . . Two more days.'

Chapter Nine

On the following afternoon Sally took Tony and Alison over to Blackett's Lane to have tea at the caravan. Eve Sherston had rung up as she'd promised, the day after their meeting, to make the arrangement, and Sally had accepted with alacrity. The children had been told about the caravan and were both eagerly looking forward to the outing.

They reached the quarry about half past three. Sally's recollections of the place were a little vague, but it turned out to be quite as pleasant as she remembered it. It was a flat, spacious semi-circle, ringed at the back and sides by a rough cliff of yellow stone which in turn was surmounted by some scattered silver birches and scrub oak. In one corner, a large horse-chestnut tree provided useful shade. The floor of the quarry was hard and dry, with patches of short turf and moss growing among the stones, and some old bits of tree boughs bleached white like the bones of animals. Near the road, where the ground was softer, a belt of thick bushes gave a curtain of privacy to the site.

Eve was sitting in a deck chair by the caravan reading a book when they arrived. At the sound of the car she waved and came smiling to meet them, greeting the children with a friendly 'Hallo!' There was no sign of George Sherston, and Eve explained that he'd gone into Bath for the afternoon. It would give Sally and herself a better chance to talk, she said, with an oddly conspiratorial air.

Once again, as Sally looked at her, she was struck by Eve's outstandingly attractive appearance. With her beautiful colouring, her dark, amused eyes, and her easy manner, it was impossible not to be drawn to her. The children took to her at once, and were fascinated when she showed them how all the bits and pieces of the caravan worked. There was a wooden shelf that let down and became an extra bunk, and for a while they were absorbed in fitting together the jig-saw of foam rubber that made up the mattress and then taking turns climbing up on to it. Afterwards Eve got them to gather sticks, and lit a fire outside the caravan to boil the kettle on – just to make it seem like real camping, she said. She'd prepared a superb tea for them inside and, altogether, was proving herself a model children's hostess.

Both Alison and Tony were looking a little somnolent by the time the last of the cakes had disappeared. Eve, casting about for something new to occupy them, said, 'Do you collect conkers, Tony?'

'You bet!' Tony said, livening up at once. 'I've got a four-hundred-and-ninety-eighter at home,' he confided. 'It's a last-yearer. It's the school conker. We have form conkers, too.'

'Well, there are no end of them under that tree over there – but I don't know whether they're ripe.'

'Oh, I'll soon tell. Come on, Alison, let's go and see . . . Can we, Mummy?'

'Of course,' Sally said. 'You can do what you like as long as you keep away from the cliff . . .' She watched them race off. For the first time, she and Eve were alone together.

'Well,' Eve said with a smile, 'now that the little pitchers are out of the way I can give you the message I've got for you. George says he's terribly sorry about last night – he realizes he was awfully rude and he hopes you'll forgive him.'

Sally looked at her blankly. 'What on earth are you talking about, Eve?'

'Why, his ringing up, of course. Obviously he ought to have spoken to one of you first – it was unforgivable. However angry he was he ought to have done that.'

Sally stared. 'You mean it was he who rang up Roscoe?'

'Why, yes . . . Didn't you know?'

'No – Roscoe didn't tell us who it was . . .' She broke off. She was beginning to understand now why Eve had had that oddly collusive air to start with. 'What was it all about?'

'Well, it was quite stupid actually. Believe it or not, Roscoe suddenly turned up here yesterday morning ... I was never so surprised in my life. He *said* he just happened to be passing, but frankly I think he'd been hanging around. Anyway, it was an odd coincidence that George was away in town making inquiries about that "cure" business – and very awkward for me afterwards. I wouldn't have mentioned it to George at all – he's terribly jealous and I knew he'd be furious about it – but Roscoe was smoking a cigarette and he came into the caravan with it, and as George and I don't smoke I knew he'd realize someone had been there. So I had to tell him, and he was mad, as I knew he would be – he rushed straight off to the phone box, and warned Roscoe to keep away.'

'Good heavens, Eve, I'm not surprised. And I don't blame him in the least ... Eve, I *am* sorry.'

'Well, it wasn't your fault, was it? Anyway, it was a lot of fuss about very little – nothing really happened, except that Roscoe got a bit fresh and I had to tell him to behave himself. I must say he's got the most colossal nerve! I didn't tell George he'd got fresh, of course, or he wouldn't have been content just to telephone ... ! What's the matter with the man – hasn't he got a girl of his own?'

'Apparently not' Sally said, 'though he obviously ought to have – he's a positive menace ... It isn't the first time this sort of thing's happened, you know. John and I got very worried about him and Kira a few days ago – she's our nice Norwegian girl – and John had to speak to him about it Now it looks as though he's switched to you. He told us he was thinking of taking a wife – but I'm afraid he's just a wolf.'

Eve smiled. 'Well, he'd better not try to take George's wife unless he's looking for trouble! George is a kind old thing at heart but he'd beat the brains out of anyone he caught making a pass at me. He was brought up rough and tough, and I'm afraid he's still not very civilized ...'

'It's Roscoe who isn't civilized,' Sally said bitterly.

Eve gave her a puzzled look. 'I agree, I think he's a terrible man – but as he's a guest in your house and a friend of yours . . .' She broke off. 'Well, it's a bit difficult.'

'He's not a friend,' Sally said. 'He's much more than that – and much less . . .' In a few words, she told Eve about the rescue incident and all that had followed it.

Eve listened, fascinated. 'Well,' she said, 'that really *is* a story . . . Now things are beginning to make sense . . . You know, George and I simply couldn't make out how Roscoe fitted into the picture – we were absolutely baffled. You and your husband seemed so charming and gentle, and we both thought Roscoe was a shocker – frightfully good-looking, of course, at least *I* thought so, but the way he behaved . . .! You should have heard George on the subject that first night – he was really livid about that crack that Roscoe made . . . I'm not surprised, either – it was a bit much, coming from a complete stranger . . . Roscoe must be an extraordinary person.'

'We can't make him out at all,' Sally said. 'Sometimes he seems quite normal – and other times he behaves like a particularly nasty delinquent. It's terribly worrying.'

'I should think so . . . What are you going to do about him?'

'Oh, we're going to tell him he'll have to go. We'd have done it before, but the thing is, he *did* save me and Tony, nothing can alter that – and John's so very conscientious . . .'

'Heavens!' Eve said. 'How conscientious can you get?'

Chapter Ten

But now even Mellanby's patience was at an end. For sheer reckless impudence he had rarely heard anything to beat Roscoe's latest escapade. The other incidents had been disturbing enough, but this was really going too far. As soon as Sally told him the news he mentally gave Roscoe one more night. He would speak to him that evening, he decided, and ask him to leave first thing in the morning.

Then something rather confusing happened. When Roscoe returned shortly after six he sought Mellanby out and humbly apologized for his behaviour of the previous day. He said that the angry telephone call had been from Sherston, and explained why it had been made. He said that he'd called at the caravan on impulse and was now thoroughly ashamed of himself. He realized that he'd behaved abominably in his host's house – indeed, that he'd been behaving badly for some time – and he was ashamed of that, too. He knew it didn't excuse him, but the fact was he'd been under a good deal of strain since he'd left the Army, worrying about how he was going to make a living. Things had got him down a bit – but from now on he'd try to do better. His manner was so chastened, his attitude so different from what it had been, that Mellanby – with some misgivings – felt he had no alternative but to wait a little longer and see what happened.

He was glad next morning that he'd done so, for the change of heart seemed genuine. Through the next two days, Roscoe's behaviour was impeccable. He was kind to the children, gentle to Kira, and as polite and considerate as anyone could wish. The sense of strain departed from the house. Relations, if not exactly cordial, were at least amicable again. Mellanby was able to concentrate on his work once more without anxiety. Eve, whom Sally had invited to tea on a return visit, said she could only suppose that Roscoe had been brought to his senses by George's sharp warning. Whatever the reason she was glad for Sally's sake that things had been patched up. When, next day, the Mellanbys gave the Sherstons lunch at a little restaurant near the Pump Room, the talk was scarcely at all of Roscoe, and almost entirely of Bath. George Sherston had been most impressed by the Roman remains they'd seen, and Mellanby, riding his hobby horse, was only too happy to discuss them. Altogether, he got on very well with Sherston. He liked his vigorous enthusiasms, and found his outspoken manner most refreshing.

Next morning a letter arrived for Roscoe – the first he'd received at the Mellanby house. The contents were evidently not to his liking, for he looked very glum during breakfast and went off in the Humber afterwards with scarcely a word. When he returned in the evening he was still brooding, and as soon as dinner was over he asked Mellanby if they could have a private talk. Mellanby took him along to the study and gave him a chair. 'What's worrying you?' he asked.

'Well, old man,' Roscoe said, 'it seems as though I'll have to take you up on that offer of a loan, after all.'

Mellanby looked at him in surprise. 'You mean you've found a place that suits you?'

'No, I haven't found anything – and unless I can raise some money quickly I'll have to give up the whole idea.'

'Why, what's the trouble?'

'Well, the fact is, I owe quite a bit,' Roscoe said. 'I hoped the chap would wait and take it a little at a time when the farm started to pay, but instead of that he's dunning me for the whole lot right away . . . That was the happy news I got in that letter this morning.'

There was a little silence. Then Mellanby said, 'How much do you owe?'

'Oh – a thousand or two . . .' Roscoe gave a rueful grin. 'Well, more than that, actually. I suppose I'd better come clean with you . . . Seven thousand pounds.'

Mellanby stared at him. 'That's a lot of money.'

'You're telling me, old man ...! Still, it wouldn't be a lot to you, would it? I mean, you're obviously well-heeled.'

'It's a lot of money by any standards,' Mellanby said.

Roscoe gave a shrug. 'I'm told you've given much more than that to charity – everyone I've talked to in the town speaks very highly of your generosity ... Well, surely I'm a more deserving cause than any charity?'

Mellanby said nothing.

'Look,' Roscoe said, 'let me put it this way ... If you'd known you could save your wife and child from drowning by paying seven thousand pounds beforehand, you'd have paid it, wouldn't you, like a shot?'

'Naturally.'

'Well, as it happens, they were saved first and now you have the chance of settling afterwards. You owe me for two lives. You've talked a great deal about gratitude. Okay – this is the pay-off.'

Mellanby looked hard at him. The change of heart was clearly over. Here was the old, offensive Roscoe back again – but this time there was something new as well. The whole situation, Mellanby felt was beginning to take a rather ugly turn.

'You put things very bluntly,' he said.

'I've got to put things bluntly. Unless I can raise this money, I'm sunk. You promised to help me, and I need help. I'm claiming it as a right.'

Mellanby took out his pipe, and lit it and puffed away quietly while he considered the position. Finally he said, 'All right Roscoe – I'll be equally blunt. I accept that I have an obligation – a big one. It's been weighing on me quite a bit. I've been waiting for an opportunity to discharge it. If you'd come to me, as I hoped you would, and said that you'd found the farm you'd been looking for and needed a few thousands to put you on your feet there, I'd have been glad to help. I still want to help – but I'd like to be quite sure I'll be doing you some real good.'

'Surely I'm the best judge of that?'

'Even so, I'd like to know a bit more ...'

'You mean you want to pry into my affairs?'

Mellanby gave a slightly sardonic smile. 'You're asking me for a present of seven thousand pounds – don't you think perhaps I'm entitled to put a friendly question or two?'

'As long as they're friendly. I don't like unfriendly questions . . .!' The old note of truculence was back. 'What do you want to know?'

'Well – who do you owe this money to?'

'Does it matter?'

'It matters to me.'

'All right,' Roscoe said sulkily. 'If you must know, he's a colonel in the RE – or was. Chap named Lancaster. He's retired now. Lives in London.'

'Would you think it prying if I asked you how you came to borrow so much money?'

'I would – but I don't mind telling you. It was three or four years ago. I was stationed in Kenya, and so was Lancaster. We were good pals. He had a private fortune, lucky chap! Anyway, I got a notion to fix myself up with a bit of property out there as a speculation – nice farmhouse. Everyone said it was bound to go up in value when we'd smashed the Mau Mau. Lancaster lent me most of the dough, and I bought it. Then the Mau Mau burned the place down! So I'd got a debt, and nothing to show for it. And that's all there is to it.'

'Wasn't the property insured?'

'Not against the Mau Mau, no. I thought it was, but it wasn't.'

'Didn't Colonel Lancaster take a mortgage on the place?'

'No, he just gave me a cheque. He was that sort of chap.'

'It was certainly a very friendly thing to do.'

'Oh, I paid him a good rate of interest, of course.'

'Out of your Army salary?'

'Sure!'

'That must have been a bit of a strain.'

'It was, but I managed it.'

'And now he's asking for the whole capital back?'

'That's right. Wants it urgently.'

'Would you have any objection to showing me the letter he wrote you?'

'Well, really . . . ! Are you calling me a liar?'

'Not at all,' Mellanby said mildly. 'It's just that I'd like to see what he says.'

'Well, I'm sorry – you can't. I was so damned annoyed about the whole thing I tore it up and threw it away. Chucked it over a hedge somewhere.'

'That's a pity . . . How did he know you were staying here, by the way?'

'I wrote to him the other day, out of pure good nature – told him I'd got promising plans and hoped to start paying off the loan pretty soon. I thought it would keep him sweet – but it merely set him off.'

Mellanby nodded. 'Of course, you could start paying him now with a part of your gratuity – it would show that you meant business . . . After twenty years' service, it must surely be quite a big lump sum?'

Roscoe gave him a long, derisive stare. Then he said, 'I'll need all that for the poultry farm.'

'You still plan to buy one?'

'Of course – once I'm in the clear again. With seven thousand pounds from you, I'll have nothing to worry about.'

Mellanby nodded again. He suddenly felt very tired. 'Tell me, what is Colonel Lancaster's exact address?'

'That's my affair, Mellanby – there's no need for you to go chasing him up. I've given you all the facts, and they're true – you can take my word for that . . . If you don't want to pay your debt, just say so.'

Mellanby tapped out his pipe and got up.

'Well . . . ?' Roscoe pressed him.

'I'll need to think about it,' Mellanby said. 'We'll talk about it again – tomorrow night.'

Chapter Eleven

First thing next morning Mellanby drove into town to check up on Roscoe's story. It went against the grain, but after what had happened he felt he had no choice. With the best will in the world, he'd been unable to believe a word of what he'd been told. It was too fantastic – the purchase of a valuable property in Kenya by a serving officer without means, the big loan made entirely on trust, the failure to insure ... And Roscoe's behaviour could hardly have been more suspicious, with his refusal of Lancaster's address, his convenient destruction of the letter, his obvious fear of inquiries. Mellanby felt practically certain that the pressing creditor was an invention. Now he intended to make *quite* certain.

The task proved to be even easier than he'd expected. In the public reference library in Bath, copies of the Army Lists dating back some time were soon dug up for him. It took him only a few minutes to discover that there had been no Colonel Lancaster of the Royal Engineers in recent years. Roscoe *had* invented him! But that was only the beginning. Until now, Mellanby had taken Roscoe's account of himself completely on trust. This seemed the moment to verify it. Quickly, he paged through the Lists, searching for a Major Frank Roscoe of the Gloucesters. There wasn't one. Roscoe had invented him, too.

For a little while Mellanby sat motionless, thinking back to the first developments in the Roscoe saga. It was difficult now to believe that anything had been above board ... Presently he left the library and drove out to the Plough at Fresney Stoke. There, over a glass of sherry, he learned from the landlord that the season had not been a good one in spite of the recent improvement in the weather, and that at no time during the summer had the Plough been without an empty room.

So there it was! – worse, much worse, than Mellanby had suspected. There could be no doubt about it now. The web of lies, the phony creditor, the request for money – everything fitted. Roscoe was a fake and a fraud. A confidence man. No wonder he hadn't wanted newspaper publicity after the rescue! He hadn't been in the Army, and it was most unlikely he'd been genuinely looking for a farm. All he'd been looking for was a victim! He'd tricked his way into the Mellanbys' home, exploiting their gratitude, watching his opportunities, intending all the time to ask for money in the end – it was a familiar story. And yet . . . Mellanby frowned. There were some very odd things about it – things that *didn't* fit . . .

Depressed and puzzled, he drove home and told Sally the result of his inquiries. She listened in shocked silence. Like Mellanby, she had been prepared for part of it – but not for all.

'What baffles me,' Mellanby said, 'is how he ever thought he could get away with it. That story of his never even *began* to sound true.'

'I suppose he was just trying it on,' Sally said.

'Do I really seem so gullible?'

'Well darling, you do give a superficial impression of not being too worldly-wise.'

Mellanby gave a grim smile. 'Even so, he must have known I'd never hand over seven thousand pounds without making some sort of check. In fact I'm sure he *did* know I made it clear enough. So where did he think he was getting . . .? He'd have done better to ask me straight out for a gift when he first came here.'

'You'd hardly have given him seven thousand pounds, even as an outright gift,' Sally said, 'without showing a little interest in what he was going to do with it – you were too anxious to help him get settled . . . He'd have known he'd be shown up as a fake in the end.'

'M'm! – perhaps you're right . . . But at least he'd have been no *worse* off – he certainly hasn't got anywhere as it is. For a confidence man, I can't imagine anything cruder than the way he's gone about things.'

'Well he's just not a very good confidence man, darling.'

'He's hopeless – I could do better myself . . .! Why did he have to say he was a major in the Gloucesters? And this mythical Lancaster – why put him in the RE? Everyone knows about the Army Lists . . . He was heading for trouble right from the start.'

Sally looked thoughtful. 'When he first told me he was in the Army, he'd only just met me, of course – he didn't know then that you had money . . . Perhaps he said the first thing that came into his head – and then had to stick to it and embroider it when he found there were prospects.'

'Does a confidence man ever say the first thing that comes into his head . . .? I still don't understand. In any case, you'd think if he'd planned to ask for money on that scale he'd have behaved a bit better, instead of going out of his way to put our backs up.'

'Well, if you ask me,' Sally said, 'he's just not quite normal. I don't mean he's mad, but no one could possibly call him well-balanced. It's the only explanation I can think of for his peculiar behaviour.'

'It's certainly the kindest one!' Mellanby said.

There was a little pause. Then Sally said, 'Anyway – what are you going to do?'

Mellanby shrugged. 'Have it out with him, I suppose. Hear what he has to say, and then tell him to clear off . . . What else can I decently do . . .? *Damn* the fellow! It was bad enough having to be grateful to him before – now it's quite intolerable . . .'

Chapter Twelve

The showdown, Mellanby realized, would inevitably be most unpleasant. Roscoe, his hopes shattered, might well become noisy and abusive when he was asked to leave. It would be the kind of undignified scene that Mellanby most detested – and certainly one to be kept as private as possible. At his suggestion, Sally took steps to see that, apart from the children, they would have the place to themselves for the evening. By good luck it was Cook's regular day off and Sally would be getting a cold meal herself, so that was all right. The daily maid always went at five. When the time came, Kira needed little persuading to let Sally bath the children while she went to see a film she'd heard was good. By a quarter to seven, Tony and Alison were both in bed, and far enough away from the sitting-room not to be disturbed. When they woke in the morning, Sally thought protectively, all the trouble would be over and they'd know nothing about it. She gave them a specially fond goodnight kiss and went downstairs to join Mellanby.

It was later than usual when Roscoe came in that evening – and he was by no means in his usual state. Normally he was most particular about his appearance, but today his clothes looked rumpled and dirty and there was a deep scratch all down his left cheek – the result, he said, with a curious jauntiness, of an encounter with a bramble while he was tramping round a field. The scratch was bleeding a little, and he went upstairs to attend to it. When he came down he joined Mellanby and Sally in the sitting-room and, as always, helped himself to a large drink.

'Where's Kira?' he asked.

'She's gone to the pictures,' Sally said.

He nodded. 'Well, Mellanby, let's get this over before dinner, shall we? What have you decided?' His tone was as confident as ever. His eyes were hard and bold. He seemed not to care at all that Sally was in the room. Looking at him, Mellanby was aware of a dislike for the man that amounted almost to hatred. He had to make an effort to speak calmly.

'I checked up on your story,' he said.

Roscoe eyed him thoughtfully. 'You did, eh . . .?' He sounded a bit disappointed, but not in the least abashed. 'Pity . . .! Still, I can't say I'm surprised . . . I didn't think you could be quite the sap you seemed to be.'

'*Really*!' Sally exclaimed. 'You don't have to be insulting as well as everything else . . .'

Mellanby put a restraining hand on her arm. 'Leave it to me, darling . . . Anyway, there it is, Roscoe. You weren't a major in the Gloucesters. There's no Colonel Lancaster. You haven't a gratuity, and I'm pretty sure you haven't been seriously looking for a farm.'

Roscoe grinned. 'You're dead right,' he said. 'What the hell would I want with a lot of damn silly hens?'

Mellanby gave a little sigh. 'Well, that seems to be that, doesn't it? At least we know where we are. I don't pretend to understand you – you've put on a pretty inept performance and I can't imagine what you think you're getting out of it all . . .'

'I'm getting seven thousand pounds,' Roscoe said.

Mellanby looked at him incredulously. 'You surely don't expect that now?'

'Indeed I do. I saved your wife and child, didn't I? I did my golden deed, and that's what it's damn well going to be – golden!'

Mellanby shook his head. 'You're wrong, Roscoe . . . I won't say our account's squared, because in a sense it never can be, but if you think I'm going to pay seven thousand pounds to a brazen crook you're making a big mistake. What I am going to do is to let you go without preferring any charge – and that'll be on my conscience, because I don't doubt you'll go off at once and try to fleece someone else . . . Still, there it is – you're free to go, and I think it would be much more comfortable all round if you went straight away.'

'Oh – you do?' Roscoe said. He struck a match on the sole of his shoe, lit a cigarette, and flung the spent match into the Adam fireplace. 'Well, now let me tell *you* something. I like it here. The house is nice and the food's adequate and it all suits me very well. With your seven thousand in the bank I shall get along fine. So I'm staying, Mellanby.' He grinned at Sally. 'I even like your wife I think I could go places with her.'

Mellanby sprang up, his face white and hard. 'You must be out of your mind . . . Get out of here!'

Roscoe settled his great bulk more comfortably in his chair. He looked as though nothing short of a crane would move him. 'You don't know me very well yet, Mellanby, do you? – but you're going to very soon. You've been underrating me, you know. I agree I'm not a top-class confidence man, but that's because it's not really my line. I try it now and again, just for a change, but I'm not much good at inventing plausible yarns, and anyway I haven't the temperament for it. If you're a confidence man you've got to behave well and be nice to people right up to the time you make your killing – and I find that difficult, as you've probably noticed! I much prefer getting what I want in other ways. More direct ways . . . Like today, for instance . . .' He fingered the long scratch on his cheek, reminiscently. 'Where do you think I was this afternoon? I'll tell you – it'll help you to understand me. I called on Eve Sherston again while her big slob of a husband was in town taking a bath. I had quite a time with her. See what I mean?'

Sally said, in a voice of horror, 'Oh, *no!*'

'Oh, *yes!*' Roscoe mimicked, 'You see, *I'm* not afraid of people. I'm not afraid of Sherston. People are afraid of me. Everybody is, when they get to know me. *You* are, Mellanby. Do you think I can't see you sweating? You know I could break you over my knee if I wanted to . . . And nobody wants to get hurt. Not *badly* hurt! People will do almost anything to avoid it. That's what I've found, anyway. It's the secret of my success.'

Mellanby was staring at him in disbelief. He *couldn't* be talking this nonsense seriously. It was preposterous – worse than the worst cheap melodrama. The man was either bluffing or crazy … Whichever it was, there was only one thing to do. Mellanby took a step towards the telephone.

Before he could reach it, Roscoe was in his path, towering over him. A large hand came out, there was a shove against his chest like the kick of an elephant, and Mellanby fell back with a crash into the chair he had just left.

'Not much use *you* trying any rough stuff, little man,' Roscoe said calmly. 'And don't you move, Sally – I'm not having any sneaking out. We're going to come to a full understanding before anybody moves.'

There was a tense silence in the room. Mellanby sat still, watching him, trying not to panic, trying to think what to do. In all his life he had never thought he'd have to cope with a situation remotely like this. Until now, violence had passed him by completely. He'd often imagined, but never known, how ugly, how terrifying it could be. His mouth felt dry, his heart was beating so fast that he could scarcely breathe. He felt horribly conscious of his own inadequacy – of Sally, who depended on him in this crisis, of the children upstairs – and of the brutal, reckless face in front of him, the face, he now recognized, of a hoodlum – a hoodlum he didn't begin to know how to deal with … Yet he'd got to do *something* …

Slowly, cautiously, he got to his feet again. 'You'll never get away with this, Roscoe,' he said. 'Surely you can see that … ?'

Roscoe stepped forward and gave him a stinging slap on the cheek. Sally sprang up with a cry and tried to reach the phone but Roscoe grabbed her and pushed her back into her chair. Mellanby struck out wildly at thè grinning face. A much harder slap started bright lights dancing before his eyes. Blood from a cut lip began to trickle down his chin. He felt dazed and sick.

'Well,' Roscoe said, 'now that you've had your little lesson, perhaps you'll agree to talk things over quietly … As far as I'm concerned, this is the position. I can't afford to have you go to the police. With my record, it's just not possible. So I'm going to see you don't. I'm going to stay here, and you're going to keep me – and you're going to keep quiet about me. You're going to pretend you *like* having me around. Is that clear? You won't be the first ones who've done it, if that's any consolation. You'll do it for the same reason the others did – because you don't want to be beaten to a pulp. Because you don't want to see your *kids* suffer – which is what'll happen if you talk.'

'They'll put you in prison,' Sally cried wildly. "You'll be there for the rest of your life . . .'

'Don't you believe it,' Roscoe said. 'They always let you out in the end – and I've got a long, *long* memory . . . Don't imagine you can get out of it that way. Sooner or later, whatever you told the police, I'd be free – and there's no protection in the world could keep your kids safe from me then. I'm speaking from experience – it once happened . . .! It wasn't at all nice for the folks concerned. Ever heard of people using *razors*? I'm warning you two – I'm a pretty hard man, with not much to lose . . . You play along with me, and we'll get on fine. If you don't, you'd better take a long last look at those two sweet children of yours, because when I've finished with them you'll hardly recognize them . . .'

'You're mad!' Mellanby said.

'Don't kid yourself, Mellanby – I'm as sane as you are. I know what I want that's all – and how to get it. A short life and a merry one, that's my motto. Take what you want while you can, and to hell with the consequences . . .'

A ring at the door-bell cut him short – a long, insistent ring. On the instant Roscoe's manner changed. He was suddenly wary. 'Who would that be?' he asked sharply. No one answered. He advanced threateningly on Mellanby. 'Come on, who is it? What have you been up to?'

'We don't know who it is,' Sally said, her voice scarcely above a whisper. 'We – we're not expecting anyone.'

The bell shrilled again, violently. Someone seemed to be leaning on it.

Roscoe jerked his head towards the door. 'Go and see, Sally –

but remember what I said about the kids. One word of all this, and they've had it. I mean that . . . Whoever it is, get rid of them.'

He waited tensely, watching Mellanby, while Sally went to the door.

Chapter Thirteen

There was the sound of a man's voice in the hall. Mellanby listened, straining his ears. Suddenly his heart began to pound. Surely he knew that voice . . .? It must be . . . It *was* . . .! As recognition came, a great wave of relief flooded over him. Whatever happened now, he had an ally – he and Sally were no longer alone . . . Then alarm returned. He needed no telling why Sherston had come. Neither, clearly, did Roscoe, who was backing defensively towards the wall. There was going to be a frightful explosion – nothing could stop it The voice in the hall was thick with anger, scarcely articulate. Mellanby could distinguish only one word – 'Roscoe!' Then the sitting-room door flew back with a crash and Sherston came in like a cyclone. His face was apoplectic, his eyes popping, his big fists clenched. He looked completely beside himself, a man obsessed. He didn't even glance at Mellanby. His gaze was riveted on Roscoe. 'So there you are . . .! Man, I'm going to break your bloody neck! I'll teach you to come pawing at my wife, you filthy goat!'

Roscoe said softly, 'Don't force me, Sherston.' He was holding his hands low in front of him, like a watchful wrestler. 'Don't try to start anything with me. You'll only wish you . . .'

The final words were lost as Sherston hurled his fifteen stone on Roscoe-in reckless fury. A wild mêlèe followed. The impetus of Sherston's assault had carried Roscoe to the ground and for a moment or two they fought there savagely, their arms and legs and bodies in constant, violent movement. Then they were half on their feet again, smashing and crashing round the room. Mellanby moved towards the phone. Before he could reach it Roscoe, breaking free, landed a jolting punch at Sherston's weakest point, his stomach, and Sherston fell back, writhing in agony.

'I warned you,' Roscoe said contemptuously. He seemed to have suffered little damage himself. He was cool, inhuman – a one-man gangster without a gun. He caught sight of Mellanby and took a light step towards him. 'Put that phone down . . .!'

Mellanby put it down.

Sherston was bent double, holding his stomach. Sally cried in a distraught voice, 'John, oh *John* . . . What are we going to do?'

Mellanby stood as though in a trance, not answering, scarcely aware of her. He seemed paralysed by Roscoe's ferocity and his own utter impotence.

Abruptly, Sherston straightened up and grabbed a wooden chair and flung himself on Roscoe again. Roscoe side-stepped and punched him twice with scientific strength. Sherston sagged under the blows. Sally gave a gasping cry. Roscoe was going in again. It would be a massacre . . . Suddenly, Mellanby grabbed a chair, too. Sherston, from the floor, cried, 'Hit him, John – *hit* him!' Roscoe swung round. 'What, you too, little man . . .?'

The diversion was brief, but it gave Sherston his chance. Now he was on his feet again. 'Both together!' he yelled. For a split second Roscoe seemed uncertain what to do. Then he turned on Sherston. Mellanby, in a red mist of fear and anger, raised the chair above his head and struck at Roscoe with all his strength. He felt the blow land. Under its impact, Roscoe staggered back. For a moment he stood swaying. Then, with a groan, he fell heavily to the floor against the fireplace.

Sherston went after him in a frenzy, his own chair raised . . . But even he could see there was no need to do anything more. Roscoe was lying in a motionless heap where he'd fallen. The fight was over.

Sherston set the chair down and wiped the sweat from his forehead with the back of his hand. 'Thanks, John . . .!' he said. He was still breathing hard from his efforts. 'Thanks a lot . . . You just about saved the day . . . He was too much for me . . .'

Mellanby had dropped to the floor beside Roscoe. He could

scarcely believe, now, that he'd done what he had. 'Do you think he's all right?' he asked anxiously.

Sherston looked at Roscoe with grim satisfaction. 'He will be – he's only knocked out ... He'll be round, soon.'

'I'll get some water,' Mellanby said. He went off rather unsteadily to the kitchen.

Sherston gazed around at the shambles of the room. 'God, what a mess ...! I'm sorry, Sally ...'

'It doesn't matter,' she said. She had sunk down on the settee, drained and exhausted by the brutal struggle. She still couldn't look at Roscoe without revulsion. 'We'll clear it up later.'

'I *had* to come,' Sherston said. 'I just couldn't wait to get my hands on him ... Do you know what he did? He came to the caravan and tried to attack Eve ...!'

'I know ...' Sally said. 'Is she all right?'

'I think so ... He'd have raped her, but she fought him off ...'

'He told us he'd been there.'

'He *told* you!'

'Yes, he boasted about it ... It's been dreadful here, George, too – we've had an absolutely ghastly time ... Thank heaven you *did* come, that's all – I don't know what would have happened ... He's been holding us prisoner – threatening us – hitting John ...'

'No ...!'

'It's true ... He was trying to get money out of us – all sorts of things ...'

'Why – the god-damned thug ...!' Sherston looked as though he'd like to set about Roscoe all over again.

At that point Mellanby returned with water and a towel and began to dash cold drops into the unconscious man's face. Roscoe moaned a little, but he still showed no sign of coming round. After a moment or two, Mellanby said, 'We'll have to do something about him, Sally ... Kira will be in soon.'

'Why don't we take him upstairs?' Sherston suggested.

Sally shuddered. 'No, no – he can't stay here ... I don't want the children to see him again. I don't want anything more to do with him.'

'I'll ring the police,' Mellanby said. 'They'll take him away.'

Sherston nodded. 'I guess that's the best thing . . .' He broke off, frowning down at the prostrate man. Roscoe's breathing was stertorous. He still hadn't moved. 'You don't think we ought to wait till he comes round, maybe? – after all, we did go for him with a couple of chairs.'

Sally said suddenly, 'John, he couldn't have meant what he said, could he – about the razor . . .? If we told the police, I mean?'

'I don't know,' Mellanby said. 'But we'll have to tell them in any case . . . We'll just have to put ourselves in their hands.'

Sherston was staring at Sally as though he hadn't heard properly. 'Did you say a *razor?*'

'Yes – he threatened to use a razor on the children if we didn't let him stay here, and give him money, and keep quiet about him . . . He said he had a long memory.'

'Oh – he was bluffing.'

'I'm not sure that he was . . . *I* think he's mad. I think he might do anything. He said he'd used a razor on some other people . . . John – I'm scared.'

'He's harmless enough at the moment, anyway,' Sherston said.

Sally looked at Roscoe, and quickly away again. 'Yes, but what about later . . .?'

'Darling,' Mellanby said, 'we've either got to keep him here for the night or call the police – one or the other . . . *I* think the best thing is to hand him over now.'

'I suppose so . . .' She looked very distressed. 'But, John, if anything happened to the children . . .! Oh, I'm so tired I can hardly think . . .'

'If you ask me,' Sherston said, 'you folks aren't in a state to make any decision right now . . . Look, what about me taking him along to the caravan for the night? – and we can decide what to do about him in the morning. You'll feel different then, I reckon.'

'Oh, if only you would . . .!' Sally began – and stopped. 'What about Eve, though?'

'It won't worry her if I sit over him with a spanner . . .! Anyway, I don't think he'll be giving any more trouble – he must have taken quite a crack.'

Mellanby looked at Sally. Her face was pale and drawn she was just about all in. 'Well, if you really don't mind having him . . .' he said hesitantly to Sherston.

'I'm sure it's the best way,' Sherston said.

'Then we'd better hurry – Kira's due back any minute . . .'

Once they'd made the decision, it didn't take them long to get Roscoe to the Chrysler, Mellanby took his legs. Sherston heaved up his shoulders. Sally held the door for them. In a few moments they were out in the drive and easing him on to the back seat. Mellanby's water treatment had begun to revive him at last. He still hadn't recovered full consciousness, but he was groaning.

'Perhaps I'd better come with you,' Mellanby said.

'Oh, there's no need to do that – you stay and look after Sally . . . I'll manage.' Sherston went round to the boot and found a spanner and put it on a ledge under the dash. 'If he gives any trouble I'll be only too happy to take care of him!'

'Will you be able to get him into the caravan?'

'We'll drag him in somehow, if he hasn't come round. Eve will help.'

Sally said, 'Is she really all right?'

'Yes – thank God . . .! A bit bruised and shocked, but I reckon she gave almost as good as she got. She's a tough girl – he didn't get far. What a swine! Men like that oughtn't to be allowed to live . . .' Sherston pressed the starter. 'Well . . .'

'It's decent of you to take him off our hands, Sherston,' Mellanby said. 'I do appreciate it . . . We've had a shocking night.'

'That's all right,' Sherston said. 'Don't worry – I'll see to everything . . . Come over in the morning some time, and we'll fix up about Mr Roscoe's future!'

Mellanby nodded. Sherston slipped the gear in, and the Chrysler moved quickly out of the drive and roared away up the road.

Mellanby put his arm round Sally's shoulder. 'Well – he's gone, darling.'

'Yes,' Sally said in a low voice. 'I only hope I never see him again.'

Chapter Fourteen

A sort of peace descended on the house after that – the peace of exhaustion. Neither Sally nor Mellanby wanted to talk about Roscoe any more that night Sally put away the cold meal she'd prepared and heated some soup, which was all either of them felt like eating. Mellanby straightened up the furniture in the sitting-room and removed a broken chair and some other bits of debris to the loft. By the time Kira returned, rather later than they'd expected, all traces of the fight had been cleared away. Sally asked her if she'd enjoyed the film and chatted to her for a moment or two, and then said 'Goodnight' without telling her anything. Tomorrow would be soon enough.

She was on the point of going to bed when the phone rang. It was Eve Sherston, in a voluble post-crisis mood. 'My dear,' she exclaimed, as soon as she heard Sally's voice, 'what an absolutely fantastic day . . .! George has just told me the whole story. Heavens, I thought *I'd* had enough to put up with, but from what George says it must have been far worse for you . . . That *man* . . .! Are you all right . . .? George says John rallied round splendidly – practically saved his life . . . you must feel quite proud of him . . . Of course, George was crazy, trying to take on a great hunk of muscle like Roscoe at his age . . . he might have been really hurt, but I think he's only bruised. He's much too impulsive – I did my best to stop him but there wasn't a hope . . . Anyway, it seems to be all over now . . . I can still hardly believe it . . .'

'I know,' Sally said, 'it's like some horrible nightmare . . . How are you, Eve – have you really got over your mauling?'

'More or less – though I feel absolutely worn out, of course . . .'

'It must have been frightful.'

'It *was* pretty awful ... He took me completely by surprise – I never thought for a moment he'd turn up again after George had warned him off or I wouldn't have let George leave me ... It wasn't even as though he were trying to make a mild pass, either – it's a bit much when a practically complete stranger starts chasing you round the bushes as though you're a Sabine woman or something ... *I* think he's one of those psychopaths, but George won't have it – he says he's just plain vicious ... George thinks hell get at least five years when all the things are totted up ...'

'I think a man like that should be shut away for good,' Sally said. 'I'm terribly grateful to you for having him, Eve ... Has he given any more trouble?'

'No – we had rather a job getting him into the van, but that's all ...'

'How is he now?'

'Well, that's actually what I'm ringing you about – George is a little bit worried about him ... He came round all right, but he keeps going off again. His pulse seems quite good and his colour isn't bad but he *is* behaving in a rather odd way ... George did wonder if we ought to get a doctor at once, but he thinks now it'll be all right to wait till morning – and Roscoe will probably be quite normal again by then. Anyway, he wanted John to know the position – so will you tell him ...?'

Of course – he's in the bath at the moment ...' Sally frowned into the phone. 'I do hope there's nothing seriously wrong.'

'So does George – he says it might be a bit awkward explaining ... But I'm sure there isn't – you could hardly have anybody tougher than Roscoe ... Anyway, there's the message.'

'All right, Eve – thanks for ringing ... I'll tell John – and of course he'll be over first thing in the morning ... I hope you manage to get some sleep.'

'Me, I'm going to take two little pills and make sure! Goodnight, Sally.'

'Goodnight, Eve.' Sally hung up, and went along to the bathroom to tell Mellanby.

He looked very concerned. 'I don't much like the sound of it,' he said. 'Do people usually go off again once they've come round?'

'I don't know – I don't see anything surprising about it ...? Anyway, John, there can't be much wrong with him if his pulse and colour are good, can there?'

'I suppose not – but it's rather disturbing ... I wonder if I ought to ring Hamley and take him round there right away?'

'Oh, darling, surely it's better to leave things to George he's the man on the spot, after all. It'll mean you'll be up all night, probably for absolutely nothing, and so will Dr Hamley. You'll have to barge in on George and Eve, who won't be expecting you – and think of the explanations! Honestly, I should wait till morning.'

'Perhaps you're right,' Mellanby said.

Chapter Fifteen

It seemed as though he had been in bed for only a few minutes when the telephone shrilled again in the hall. He shot up in alarm, his nerves jangling, and switched on the light above his head. The time by his watch was a quarter to three! Sally, in her own bed, was dead to the world and hadn't stirred. Mellanby slipped on his dressing gown, switched the light off again, and went quickly downstairs to take the call there. His heart was thumping. A ring at that hour could only mean trouble.

He snatched up the receiver in the sitting-room, cutting off the devilish din. 'John Mellanby here,' he said.

'John – this is George Sherston.' The familiar voice was rough with agitation. 'I'm afraid I've got bad news for you.'

'Roscoe . . .'

'Yes . . . Something frightful's happened – you'd better brace yourself . . . John – he's dead!'

'*No* . . .!' The word was a long-drawn-out whisper of horror.

'I'm afraid so . . .'

Mellanby fought the choking constriction in his throat. 'But – *how* . . .? You said he was all right . . .'

'I thought he was . . . It's one hell of a thing, isn't it?'

'I just can't believe it . . .'

'*I* couldn't believe it at first – I thought he must be in a coma . . .'

Mellanby clutched at the straw. 'Couldn't he be?'

'No, he's dead as a duck . . . No doubt about it.'

'God . . .' Mellanby took the phone and slumped into a chair with it. 'What happened . . .? When did you find out?'

'About half an hour ago. I'd been for a bit of a stroll round the van – couldn't rest. He seemed all right when I left him – he was breathing lightly, but I didn't think there was anything to worry about Then when I got back and took another look he didn't seem to be breathing at all. And he wasn't ... That knock must have smashed his skull in.'

Mellanby groaned. 'George – *why* didn't we get a doctor right away!'

'I know, we ought to have done – but who the hell would have dreamt he'd go out like that? His skull must be as thin as paper ... Probably a doctor couldn't have done much for him, anyway ... Well, there it is, John – we've been landed with this thing and now we've got to face it ... We're in a bit of a spot – but we can handle it all right ... Listen, does anyone else know what happened at your house tonight? Did you tell Kira?'

'No ...'

'Thank heaven for that! What about the children – did they hear anything?'

'I don't think so – they slept right through it ...'

'Fine ... ! I've got things pretty well sorted out at this end – I'm taking care of everything. I'd like you to come round, though – we must talk.'

'I'll come straight away.'

'Don't make any more row than you can help when you leave ... Okay, I'll be seeing you. Keep your chin up.' There was a click as Sherston rang off.

Mellanby put the receiver down in a kind of daze. For a moment or two he continued to sit there, staring in front of him. It was hard to grasp that Roscoe was dead. It was harder still to grasp that *he* – John Mellanby – had killed him. *He*, of all people ...! But it had happened, and George was right – now it had got to be faced.

Presently he went upstairs to wake Sally.

Chapter Sixteen

Twenty minutes later Mellanby was on his way to the caravan in the Humber. He was usually a rather slow driver, because of his gammy leg, but tonight he drove as fast as he could, to get to the scene quickly, to get the ordeal over. His face had lost its dazed expression. His look now was that of a man whose mind was at war with itself – a grim mask covering an inner turmoil. His thoughts kept reverting to that moment of violent impact when he'd struck Roscoe with the chair. The trouble was, he couldn't remember much about it. He hadn't been in any state to notice details at the time. He could remember how he'd felt, that was all . . . Only too well!

It took him less than half an hour to reach the quarry through the quiet lanes. A light was burning in the caravan. Eve Sherston was standing in the open doorway, silhouetted against the light as she gazed out Mellanby swung the car in beside the Chrysler, doused his lamps, and limped over to her.

'Hallo, Eve . . .' He glanced apprehensively into the van. There was no sign of Sherston. 'Where's George?'

'Over there in the bushes,' she said. Her voice had a note of panic in it. 'Oh, John, I'm so glad you've come . . . He says he's doing the best thing, but . . .'

Mellanby swung round, following the direction of her pointing finger. There was a faint glow from the vegetation near the verge of the road. He crossed the quarry and plunged into the bushes, thrusting the foliage aside. At a spot close to the road's edge, but well screened from it Sherston was wielding a spade by the light of an electric hand lamp set on the ground. There was a long, deep hole at his feet and he was feverishly shovelling earth back into it. Sweat was rolling down his face in streams. He paused for a second as Mellanby appeared, said, 'Good man! – you've been quick,' and went on shovelling.

'George – what the hell are you doing?' Mellanby cried.

'What does it look like?' Sherston said, throwing in another spadeful of earth and roots.

With incredulous horror, Mellanby gazed down. Three feet below the surface of the ground, he could just make out the death-pale face of Frank Roscoe. The scratch on the cheek showed like a dark line. The eyes were closed . . . Then a spadeful of earth covered it.

'Stop!' Mellanby shouted. He seized Sherston's arm. 'For God's sake, George, are you mad? We can't do this.'

'Quiet, man . . .!' Sherston jerked himself free and continued to shovel in the earth. 'What else can we do?'

'We can tell the truth,' Mellanby cried, in a near-frenzy. 'We *must* . . .! What's got into you?' He tried to grab the spade, but Sherston pushed him aside – not roughly, but firmly, as though his mind were made up. 'Let me finish, John – it'll be light in half an hour . . . I tell you we had no choice. We'll argue it out when I'm through.' He was beginning to stamp the soil down now. The job was almost done.

Sick with horror, Mellanby turned away. For the second time that night he felt himself utterly inadequate. Groping blindly, he stumbled back to the caravan. 'Give me a drink, Eve, for God's sake,' he said.

She poured him whisky, a stiff shot, and he drank it neat.

'George is mad,' he said. '*Mad!*'

'I tried to stop him, John, but he wouldn't listen to me. He said he knew best . . . He made me help him – it was ghastly . . . John, I'm terrified.'

'You've good reason to be . . . We all have! If only I'd *known* . . .!'

He stopped abruptly as a beam of light suddenly lit up the lane. Eve called out in alarm, 'George! – there's someone coming!' Sherston called something back and the glow disappeared from the bushes.

Eve pulled the caravan door shut and turned out the gas lamp. The sound of a car engine grew louder. Eve, a frightened voice in the darkness, said, 'Who'd come along here at this hour?' Mellanby didn't answer. He was beyond caring who came – he'd almost have welcomed someone ... The lights grew brighter. The car seemed to slow. Then it went on again. As it passed, Mellanby caught the clink of bottles. 'Milk!' Eve said, with a hysterical little laugh. 'Would you believe it ...?' When the engine noise had died she opened the door and lit the gas again. Her face was as pale as parchment under the glare.

In a few moments, Sherston appeared at the door. 'False alarm, eh?' he said to Eve. 'That thing had me worried for a second ...' He threw his spade under the caravan and wiped his hands on a rag. 'Well, that's that,' he said grimly.

He climbed into the van and pulled the door shut. 'Sorry if I was a bit rough out there, John, but I had to finish what I'd started ... Okay, I know what you're going to say – I ought to have consulted you first.'

'Of course you ought!'

'Well, it's too bad I couldn't but there just wasn't time for a lot of discussion – I had to use what darkness there was left.'

'Why do it at all? We're not criminals. We didn't kill Roscoe on purpose. It was – it was an accident ...'

Sherston poured himself a glass of water and drank deeply. Then he sat down opposite Mellanby. 'Now listen to me, John,' he said quietly. 'I've had a bit longer to think about this than you have, and I reckon I've got the position a good deal clearer ... Of course it was an accident – we neither of us intended to kill him. But I damn well intended to half-kill him if I could, and from the way you went for him I wouldn't say you were exactly friendly. Face it, man we both hated his guts, and we had good reason to. He was an out-and-out bastard, and we both knew it. So what would it look like if tonight's story got out ...?'

'I don't care what it looks like,' Mellanby said angrily.

'You soon would! Can't you see we wouldn't have a dog's chance? We both went for him with chairs, and between us we knocked him unconscious. We didn't call a doctor. Instead, we smuggled him out here, and he died. I know there was a damn good reason for everything we did, but would anyone else think so? Don't kid yourself! There's not a jury that wouldn't bring it in as manslaughter.'

Mellanby looked from Sherston to Eve, and back again. 'We only did what we were forced to do,' he said. 'Anyone who knew the facts would agree. He was too much for us you said that yourself. And there couldn't have been greater provocation. Threatening to use a razor . . .!'

'He hadn't *got* a razor though,' Sherston said. 'He hadn't got a darned thing. That's what a jury would pick on. We weren't either of us in actual danger of our lives, not at that moment with the two of us tackling him together. A jury would say we ought to have done without the chairs . . . Look, I've no qualms about what we did, don't think that – he was a louse, even if he did manage to do one good deed, and I'm shedding no tears for him. He deserves to be in that hole I've just dug, and I'm glad he's there. All I'm saying is that if the truth gets out, you and I will be jailed as criminals – and I'm damned if I'm going to lose my freedom for a bastard like that. I'm fifty-five, and my last years are precious to me . . . I tell you, man, there was only one way to look after ourselves, and that was to stick him in the ground – which is what I've done.'

'You were wrong,' Mellanby said. 'You've put us both in the wrong – hopelessly. What you've done now *is* criminal.'

'Maybe it is, technically, but not any other way – not morally. Anyhow, why should you worry? I did it on my own. I'm not asking you to take responsibility for it.'

'I *know* about it – that's enough.'

'Well, try and forget it John . . . If you can't do that just keep quiet about it!' Sherston looked grim. 'As a matter of fact I don't see how you can do anything else, now Roscoe's underground . . . They'd never believe you hadn't had a hand in it.'

Mellanby groaned. 'God – what a *mess!*'

'It's nothing like the mess it might have been?'

'You can't be sure of that,' Mellanby said, 'How do you know the whole thing won't come out? Then where would we be?'

Sherston shook his head. 'How can it? – who's to know? All you have to do is give out that Roscoe didn't like the Bath district after all and pushed off somewhere else – you don't know where – and that'll be that . . . He hadn't any roots here. He hadn't any friends, had he? I wouldn't think so! Who's going to search for him? He came here out of the blue, and he's gone back into it.'

'It's not as simple as that' Mellanby said. 'Everyone leaves traces . . . What about his things up at the house – his clothes . . .?'

'Well, you'll have to pack those up double-quick – hide them somewhere tonight and bring them along here as soon as you get the chance. I'll soon get rid of them.'

Mellanby glanced out of the window. The sky had the pale look of dawn – the bushes by the road were taking shape. The quietness of death lay over the quarry. He shivered. 'Suppose someone found him . . .? A dog might . . .' He broke off, unable to finish.

'You needn't worry,' Sherston said. 'He's four feet down and well stamped on . . . By the time I've finished with the place, there won't be a trace. In a week or two it'll be grown over. Nobody's going to find him, and nobody's going to suspect a thing. I'm certain of that.'

'It's so incredibly cold-blooded . . .'

'John, this isn't a time to be squeamish. I know how you feel – right now I'm pretty queasy myself, to tell you the truth, though God knows I've seen tougher things done in my time, *and* done them . . . The thing is, it was necessary.'

'Eve doesn't think so.'

'I didn't at first,' Eve said, 'but now I think George is right . . . Why should we risk ruining our lives for a man like Roscoe?'

Mellanby got to his feet. 'Well – I don't know . . . I'll have to think about it. I must talk to Sally.'

'You do that,' Sherston said. 'Talk to Sally. Ask her if she wants *her* life ruined. Shell say I'm right – you'll see . . .' He got up and opened the door. 'I'm sorry about this, John. You're a man of principle, much more than I am . . . I know what it means to you,

I know it's a heck of a problem. All I can say is, I've tried to do my best – for both. I honestly couldn't see any other way.'

Mellanby nodded. His face was grey and set. 'I'll come back later, anyway.'

'With the clothes!' Sherston called after him. 'And, John – be careful! Watch your step!'

Chapter Seventeen

Sally said, with an effort at calmness, 'The thing is, John, what *would* happen if you told the truth? Do you think George is right or wrong?'

It was an hour later. The gruesome news of Roscoe's summary disposal, added to the shock of his death, had quite shattered Sally at first, but the problem of what to do next was so urgent that she'd forced herself to put the horror out of her mind and concentrate on the dilemma that faced them. No decisions had been taken yet, but as a precaution – and to Mellanby it seemed halfway to a decision – Sally had gathered all Roscoe's belongings together and locked them away in a cupboard. Kira and the children were still asleep – but they wouldn't be much longer. They'd have to be told something. The question was, what? Sally and Mellanby, facing each other in the bedroom in a state of desperate anxiety, now had to make up their minds.

It was a little while before Mellanby answered. On his way back from the caravan he'd had time to do some hard thinking. He had to be honest with Sally, but he hated having to tell her his conclusions. When at last he replied, it was as though the words were being dragged from him one by one.

'I'm horribly afraid George may be right,' he said.

Sally looked at him blankly. 'You mean you *would* be sent to prison!'

'I think it's quite likely,' Mellanby said. 'I didn't to begin with, but I do now ... Of course, it's hard to be certain – so much would depend on the judge – but I've been thinking about other cases and they're not very reassuring ... Do you remember that man in Bristol last year? – Ferguson, I think his name was. He attacked his wife's lover and they fought and the man died . . . He'd had much more to put up with than George or I – but *he* was sent to prison . . . So why should we get off . . .? You see, Sally, we did take the law into our own hands. George could have gone to the police in the first place instead of rushing round here to try and beat Roscoe up. They'll say that's what he ought to have done . . . And I could have slipped out and rung the police when Roscoe was hitting George, instead of joining in . . . The truth is, we were both completely beside ourselves and went for him blindly – and the law will say we used more than the necessary force.'

'But, John, it was sheer bad luck that he died.'

'For him *and* for us!'

'If he hadn't done, no one would have given it another thought . . .'

'I know,' Mellanby said, 'The trouble is, the law goes mainly by results.'

'I suppose so . . . But, darling, surely it would weigh with a judge and jury that Roscoe was such a ghastly man. The way he behaved from the beginning – all those horrible threats – and attacking Eve like that . . .'

'Well . . .' Mellanby hesitated. 'They might see things a bit differently . . . You see, they'd only have our version – and it might be hard to convey just why we felt so terrorized. They might think that Roscoe's threats were pretty fantastic and that it would have been perfectly safe to pretend to play along with him and go to the police afterwards. They might easily think I just lost my head . . . The attack on Eve is another matter, but there again they might wonder just how serious it was. Eve's taken it much more lightly than George, and she doesn't seem to have any marks on her . . . I'm sure all these things *would* weigh, particularly if Roscoe turned out to have a bad police record – but they wouldn't be enough. He still had the right to live.'

'I can't believe a jury wouldn't be sympathetic, all the same,' Sally said.

Mellanby shook his head. 'There's another side to that, too, I'm afraid ... There's such a thing as forfeiting sympathy. Have you thought what sort of figure I'd cut in the box ...? Roscoe was a man who'd risked his life to save you and Tony from drowning – I owed him everything – and a few days afterwards I bashed him with a chair. It doesn't sound very pretty, does it? And that's only the beginning. We didn't do any of the things we ought to have done after it happened. We didn't call a doctor, or the police – as George says, we smuggled him out. We can explain all that after a fashion, but whatever we say it'll *look* as though we were trying to cover up, as though we felt guilty ... And then – *burying* him ...! Even if we got over the other things, we'd never get over that. It was an appalling thing to do – it would put any jury against us ... No, Sally, I think we've got to face it – the verdict would be manslaughter, and we'd get anything up to five years.'

'Five years ...! *John!*'

'It's happened to others. It could just as easily happen to us.'

'But it would be so utterly unjust – you've done absolutely nothing to deserve it ... Five *years!*' Sally gazed at Mellanby with frightened eyes. 'It's unthinkable ... Darling, it would mean the end of everything, it would destroy our lives. We'd never get over it – we couldn't! ... And think of Tony and Alison ... John, it's just too awful ...'

Mellanby was silent.

Presently Sally said, in a different tone, 'And suppose we keep quiet about it all – what then?'

Mellanby gave a little shrug. 'I imagine George is probably right about that, too ... I don't see why Roscoe's body should ever be found. If we say that he left here last evening, while Kira was out and the children were asleep, nobody's going to disbelieve us ... Of course, if inquiries ever did start things might get very difficult ...'

'Are they likely to?'

'Well you never know – something might start them off. But at the moment I can't think of anything that would.'

There was another little silence. Then Sally said slowly, 'So it comes to this – if we tell the truth, we probably ruin our lives, and if we don't there's a good chance we can carry on as though ...' She hesitated.

'As though nothing had happened?' Mellanby said, with rare bitterness.

'No, darling, of course not – I know things would never be the same again – but at least the children wouldn't suffer ... After all, John, we can't bring Roscoe back to life. What *good* would you be doing by telling the truth? What would you be doing it *for?*'

'For myself, I suppose,' Mellanby said. 'I dare say it's very old-fashioned of me, but I happen to be a law-abiding man. I *believe* in law and order. I don't believe people are entitled to disregard the law and make their own rules just because it happens to suit them. I've a very deep feeling about it.'

'Well, yes, I know,' Sally said, 'and I do agree with you, of course ... But there must be exceptions sometimes.'

'I wouldn't think so.'

'John, you've made exceptions yourself ... What about when you found out Roscoe was a confidence man? – you were going to let him go because you were grateful to him, instead of handing him over to the police. You were making your own rules then.'

Mellanby pondered. 'Yes ... Strictly speaking, I suppose I was wrong ... But at least I wasn't doing it to shield myself, which is what I'd be doing now.'

'But, darling, if the law's stupid and unjust ...'

'It doesn't matter, Sally – it's the only thing there is between us and the jungle. It's the only thing that makes a decent, civilized life possible. If people were allowed to ignore it because they'd got good reasons, that would be the end of organized society – and soon we'd all have to carry bludgeons. Either you have laws and observe them, or in the long run you're sunk.'

'I don't see how one could be more sunk than having to do five years in jail for absolutely nothing!'

'That depends ... What do you think the five years would be like *out* of jail?'

Sally gazed at him unhappily. 'You really *want* to confess, don't you?'

'I hate the thought of living with a lie all my life. I hate it more than I can tell you.'

'More than prison?'

'I think so ... I'd much prefer to tell the truth and take the consequences.'

'Tony and Alison would have to take the consequences too, darling. Their young lives would be pretty well blasted ... Isn't it possible that confession would be a bit of a self-indulgence?'

'I don't know ... I suppose it would ...' Mellanby passed a hand wearily over his face. 'Who said, the path of duty was strait and narrow? It's so wide you can get lost in it ... Honestly, Sally, I don't know *what* we should do.'

There was a little silence. Then Sally said, with deep conviction, 'Well, *I* do, darling – I think we should keep quiet. I know how you feel, and I respect you for it but I think this is a case where you've simply got to sit on your feelings ... You've done nothing wrong, you don't have to have a conscience about anything, and if you've got to live with a lie it's not a lie you need be ashamed of ...'

'I wonder,' Mellanby said.

'You *know* it isn't ... Darling, I'm absolutely certain that your duty is to say nothing – if only for the sake of the children. Quite frankly, I don't think you've the right to do anything else.'

There were sounds on the landing as she finished – Kira's voice, a high-pitched laugh from Alison, the pounding of feet. The day had begun. Sally said, in an urgent tone, 'John, we've got to decide ... *Please!*'

Mellanby got up from the bed. His face was expressionless. 'Very well,' he said. 'We'll take Roscoe's things along to George and he can dig another hole.'

Chapter Eighteen

Sally had to wait for a suitable moment to tell Kira and the children that Roscoe had left. It would be a mistake, she decided, to rush and announce the fact right away, as though it were the only thing on her mind; she must tell them soon, but it must come naturally. As it turned out the perfect opportunity presented, itself when she went down to the kitchen. There was the fragrant smell of coffee in the air – breakfast was under way. As she entered, she heard Kira say, 'Alison, please ask Uncle Frank if I shall boil an egg for him . . .'

'Uncle Frank's gone,' Sally said, 'he left last night . . .' As three faces turned to her in surprise, she added, 'He was very sorry not to have a chance to say goodbye, but he had to make up his mind in rather a hurry . . . He asked me to say goodbye to you all for him . . .'

Kira said, 'He has stopped looking for a farm . . .?'

'He heard of one in Sussex, Kira – that's south of London – and he thought he'd better go along right away and see it . . . He thinks he'll prefer Sussex.'

'Is he coming back?' Tony asked.

'No, I don't think so, darling.'

'But, Mummy, he's left his boxing gloves and punchball . . . They're in the shed – I just saw them.'

Sally said, 'Oh . . .!' She wondered how many other things they'd overlooked. Not that it really mattered, as long as they weren't things he'd obviously need. 'Well, if he wants them I expect he'll send for them . . . We can't write because we don't know where he is.'

'Perhaps he'll forget,' Tony said hopefully. 'It's a good punchball.' He went off into the dining-room with Alison, who seemed to have taken the loss of Uncle Frank with complete unconcern.

Sally said, 'Frank was very sorry not to see you before he went, Kira . . . I'd have told you last night when you came in but you looked a bit tired and I thought it might – well – upset you a little.'

Kira gave a faint smile. 'I am not upset.'

'I thought you rather liked him . . .'

'At first I liked him – but not later. He was not a nice man, I think. He was not sympathetic . . . I shall not cry.'

'I'm very glad,' Sally said.

'Will you have a boiled egg?'

'No, thank you – just coffee.' Sally turned away. Duplicity was as foreign to her as to Mellanby – particularly where the children were concerned. It had been a hateful conversation. But at least one ordeal was over.

The real strain, though, was still to come. Worn out after their appalling night both Sally and Mellanby now had to maintain an outwardly cheerful aspect and behave as though nothing unusual had happened. The main burden of the deception at home inevitably fell on Sally. Mellanby had already made an appointment for that morning to discuss the details of an archaeological television programme with the curator of the local museum, and with some reluctance he went off at ten to keep it. He had scarcely left the house when the telephone started to ring. The first call was from a Bath estate agent, with an urgent message for Mr Roscoe about a likely property. Sally had to tell him that Roscoe had given up the Bath district and departed to look elsewhere. The agent seemed surprised, but he was quite philosophical about it and apologized for troubling her. Then, about eleven, Eleanor Bryce rang up for a chat, and in the course of the conversation she asked if Roscoe had had any luck with his search, and Sally had to repeat her story. Finally, just before noon, Sherston telephoned to see if all was well. Sally discreetly assured him there was nothing to worry about, and said that she and Mellanby would be along as soon as they could.

In the afternoon Sally packed Kira and the children off to the park. Directly they'd gone, Mellanby whisked Roscoe's suitcase into the car while Sally kept an eye on cook and the 'daily' in the kitchen. Once in the privacy of the garage, Mellanby went carefully through the contents of the case. There might be some letters or papers, he thought, referring to appointments or commitments – things that could lead to inquiries later. But there was nothing of that kind at all – only clothes and other personal effects. He re-packed everything, and went in to tell Sally he was ready. A few minutes later they were on their way to the caravan.

It was a sombre meeting with the Sherstons. Awareness of the grave in the bushes hung over everyone like a pall. Eve, suffering badly from reaction, seemed a bundle of nerves. Sherston was grim. There was nothing anyone wanted to talk about but Roscoe, and once Mellanby had confirmed his intention to keep his own counsel, there were only a few practical things to discuss. Mellanby briefly reported on the domestic position. Then, while Sally and Eve rested in the caravan and tried to give each other comfort and reassurance, Sherston took Mellanby back to the burial place. 'I'd like you to see for yourself that there's nothing to worry about,' he said.

Deep in the bushes, Mellanby gazed down in horrid fascination at the spot. There was no doubt that Sherston had done an efficient job. Where the hole had been, the ground was now quite level, with nothing to catch the eye, nothing at all to distinguish it from the surrounding area. Sherston had skilfully drawn some trailing brambles over the place, and scattered some leaves. Soon, more leaves would fall, completely covering the grave. Mellanby gave a brief nod, trying not to think of what the hole contained.

'Where will you bury the suitcase?' he asked.

'Right here beside the body – it's the only place in the quarry where the ground's soft enough. I'll shove it in just as it is.'

'Be careful, won't you . . .? If you were seen . . .!'

'You bet I'll be careful. I'll wait till it's dark, and Eve will keep watch . . . Don't worry.'

Mellanby nodded again, 'What are your plans, George?'

'Well, I thought we'd move on tomorrow – Eve can't wait to

get away. Neither can I, for that matter. This place has kind of lost its charm!'

'I should think so . . .! Where will you make for?'

'The Continent, in the end – but we'll stick around in England till we're sure there's not going to be any trouble . . . If anything did crop up, of course, we'd need each other like hell – but I'm pretty certain it won't . . . Short of that, I reckon the less we see of each other, the better. I'll give you a ring in a week or two, just to check up with you that everything's okay . . .' He looked a little anxiously at Mellanby. 'I hope you don't still blame me, John. I guess I *was* a bit high-handed . . .'

'No, I don't blame you,' Mellanby said. 'If you'd consulted me, I doubt if I'd have agreed – but I don't know . . .? There are pressures . . . Anyway, that's academic now. I've accepted the position, and I shall go through with it.'

'Good man . . .!' Sherston gave a rather wry smile. 'You're a bit of a dark horse, John, aren't you . . .? Gentle exterior, but as tough as hell inside.'

'I wish that were true,' Mellanby said.

'Tough enough, anyway . . . Well, I hope we'll be able to meet again somewhere, all of us, when everything's blown over. It's been a rotten business – messed up a promising friendship, among other things. I can tell you Eve's going to miss Sally a lot . . . You know John, although Roscoe's dead and buried, I *still* hate his guts!'

Chapter Nineteen

The Sherstons left the district early next day, after a final telephone call to say that the suitcase had been safely disposed of and to wish Sally and Mellanby the best of luck. With their departure, the active phase of the Roscoe affair seemed to be over. There was still plenty to worry about, but nothing more to do. On the surface, at least the Mellanby household reverted to normal. Sally resumed her usual holiday activities with the family. Mellanby, with a conscious effort of will, forced himself to return to his writing. Kira, to all appearances, was cheerful and content. The children were happy, and Tony's occasional references to Uncle Frank were matter-of-fact and free from nostalgia. No one else showed any interest in what had happened to Roscoe – he had left, and that was that. As far as danger was concerned, it seemed to Sally that the whole thing had already blown over.

She felt a good deal of anxiety on other grounds. By tacit agreement she and Mellanby had virtually stopped talking about Roscoe, but she knew that he thought about the dead man even more then she did. After what had happened, she doubted if either of them would ever completely recapture their old, unclouded happiness – though with only two or three days gone since Roscoe's death, it was really too early to look into the future. For the moment, the important thing was that the family was intact, and that John was a free man. As long as he was free, there was hope.

Then, on the morning of the fourth day, a letter arrived for Roscoe – postmarked 'London, N.1' and addressed in a precise and rather elegant hand. It was Mellanby who picked it up. With feelings not unlike the foreboding he'd had when the telephone had rung on the fatal night, he opened it and read it. It was as follows:

Flat 23, Highgate 031
Egham Court
London,
N1

Dear Roscoe,

I was surprised and distressed at the contents of your second letter, which I found waiting for me when I returned here today. The money I gave you was specifically for investment in the company, and as I gather you have not yet closed the deal it should still be in your possession *in full*. You certainly had no right at all to use any part of it for your own purposes – which, judging from your evasive tone, I begin to think you must have done. Indeed, I am now seriously wondering whether the company ever existed, and whether perhaps I was not taken in by a smooth talker! If I am wrong about this I shall be only too happy to apologize – but I don't mink I am. I feel very worried and upset – and *angry*. I have been very patient, but now my patience is exhausted. The purpose of this letter is to tell you that I expect the return of the £7,000 in full and *immediately*. I will accept no excuses. If I do not receive your cheque by first post on Friday morning, I shall go at once to the police and ask for your apprehension on a charge of false pretences and fraud. In view of our past relationship I deeply regret this, but you have left me with no alternative.

Charles E. Faulkner

Chapter Twenty

Mellanby went straight to his study and dropped into a chair. The contents of the letter had hit him like a blow between the eyes. Since Roscoe's death there had always been a possibility that something awkward might turn up, but the crisis they were now suddenly plunged into was more acute and dangerous than anything he had imagined. It didn't help that he probably ought to have foreseen it. The danger had been signalled with that first letter Roscoe had received, and Mellanby blamed himself fiercely for not having given it more thought, once Colonel Lancaster had been exposed as an invention. After all, *someone* had written an upsetting letter. Roscoe's story about Lancaster had been bogus, but his anxiety hadn't been. A crook from top to toe, he *had* owed seven thousand pounds which he couldn't repay – but he'd owed it to this man Faulkner. And now everything was plain. That first letter, the one he'd so wisely thrown away, had no doubt asked for the money back – or at least for some accounting. Roscoe, desperate to stave off the reckoning, had first come to Mellanby with his phony story and his appeal for help – and when that hadn't worked he'd resorted to crude menace ... The driving force behind his fantastic behaviour was suddenly clear ... What wasn't clear was how this new and appallingly imminent danger was to be met ...

Mellanby was still groping for an answer when Sally came in search of him. His withdrawal at so early an hour was unusual, and she'd guessed that something had happened. She glanced over his shoulder at the letter, 'What is it, John? – bad news?'

'Very bad, I'm afraid.' He passed it to her.

She read it through twice, slowly.

'So he did owe money,' she said, in a flat voice.

'Yes.'

'And if this man Faulkner tells the police about him, I suppose they'll come here?'

'They're bound to. Straight here. It was Roscoe's last known address.'

Sally looked at the letter again. 'He says Friday. Friday is tomorrow!'

'Yes.'

'John! – what will you tell them?' There was panic in her voice now. 'You said if inquiries ever started . . .'

Mellanby nodded. 'It's still true – we simply can't afford any inquiries. Imagine the questions they'd ask . . . Where did he say he was going to? Did he go by train? What train did he catch? Did he take a taxi or did you drive him to the station? Did you see him off? What luggage had he? How was he dressed? Did you know he was a crook? Did he try to borrow any money from you? How did you get on with him . . .? And so on. All of them awkward. All of them full of pitfalls.'

'I can see they'd be awkward,' Sally said, 'but surely we could make up a watertight story between us . . . He told us he was going to Sussex but he didn't tell us where – that's what we've said already . . . He hadn't a car so of course he'd have had to go by train. He caught the eight o'clock to London. You drove him to the station. He was wearing his grey suit and carrying his brown case. You didn't wait to see him off. You hadn't very much liked him – you'd have to say that because Kira would know – but you didn't realize he was a crook . . . Wouldn't that be all right? After all, I don't see why they should suspect *us* of anything.'

'They wouldn't at first, Sally, but it wouldn't be long before they did . . . They'd start by checking up on his movements, to make sure he really did go to London. They'd go to the station and they'd find that no one had seen him. With a man as striking as Roscoe, that would seem pretty odd. They'd talk to the porters in the yard and discover that no one had seen my car. They'd come back and ask more questions and probably tangle us up. It isn't as though we're used to this sort of thing – we'd be caught in a web in no time ... Whatever story we told, they'd be able to disprove it. Then they'd really start ferreting around. They'd question the neighbours. Someone might have heard me drive off in the early hours. They'd want to know where I went, and why. They'd find out about the caravan ...'

'Only if you told them.'

'They'd get on to it anyway, Sally, sooner or later ... Jack Reed saw Roscoe there when he went along with the breakdown van – so did his men ... And people talk. The police would soon discover the connection. When they found that Roscoe had completely disappeared, they'd investigate everything – they'd never let go ... Honestly, Sally, it's madness to think along these lines – especially after we've kept quiet so long. If the facts were to come out now, George and I might really be finished. The charge could easily be murder ...'

Sally stared at him, white-faced. 'Then what *are* we going to do?'

'Well, I've been thinking ... Somehow we've got to stop the police coming, and I believe I know how it might be done. I'll have to see Faulkner, and I'll have to see him today ...' Briefly, he told Sally what was in his mind. 'Is his telephone number on the letter?'

'Yes – Highgate 031.'

'Then I'll ring him right away,' Mellanby said. 'If he's a decent chap, it may work.'

Chapter Twenty-One

It was close on three o'clock that afternoon when Mellanby's taxi drew up outside the modern block of flats in Highgate where Charles Faulkner lived. Flat 23, the porter told him, was on the third floor. Mellanby walked up, drawing out the last moments before the fateful interview. It wasn't that he hadn't a perfectly clear plan in his mind – the long journey up from Bath had given him plenty of time to decide what he was going to say. It was just that such guile was hopelessly out of character for him. Every word was going to stick in his throat His expression was strained as he touched the bell.

The door was opened by an elderly, rather frail-looking man, with a deeply lined face and snow-white hair. For a moment he inspected his visitor through the upper lenses of a pair of bifocals. 'Mr Mellanby?' he said. His voice was cultured, and much more vigorous than his appearance.

Mellanby nodded.

'Do come in, won't you . . .' Faulkner turned and led the way into a small but pleasantly-furnished sitting-room with a fine open view. There was an attractive seascape on the wall opposite the window, and below it, on a little table, a three-master in a bottle. 'You'll find that chair quite comfortable . . .' Mellanby sat down, with a word of thanks. The old man took a chair opposite him. There was something almost spinsterish about his prim neatness, yet in an odd way he had an air of authority. 'Well, now – you said you wanted to talk to me about Frank Roscoe. What is it, Mr Mellanby?'

Mellanby came straight to the point. 'Roscoe has been staying at my home in Bath for a week or two as my guest' he said. 'This morning he showed me a letter he'd just received from you. I gather he owes you seven thousand pounds.'

'He does, indeed.'

'Well – I've come to settle his debt.'

The old man blinked. 'You mean – Roscoe has sent the money?'

'No. I mean that I should like to pay it for him.'

Faulkner stared at him in astonishment. 'Why on earth should you do that?'

'It's very simple, Mr Faulkner . . . You see, just over two weeks ago Frank Roscoe saved my wife and small son from drowning, at the risk of his own life . . .'

'Really?'

'You'll appreciate that it's put me under an enormous obligation to him. Now I feel I have a chance to discharge the debt.'

'Well, this is *most* surprising . . .' For a moment Faulkner gazed hard at Mellanby, his eyes shrewd behind their glasses. Then he gave a slow, disapproving headshake. 'I can understand how you feel, of course – but I'm bound to say I think it would be a most quixotic action. You say he showed you my letter, so you must know my view of him . . . I'm very much afraid the man's a complete rogue.'

'Oh, he's a rogue, all right' Mellanby said. 'But in an odd sort of way that's an additional reason why I'm so anxious to square my account with him. It isn't at all pleasant to be deeply indebted to a rogue.'

'No I can imagine that . . . But believe me, Mr Mellanby, he doesn't deserve your consideration . . . He's a fraud, an utter scoundrel. He's behaved abominably to me . . .'

'How did you come to know him?' Mellanby asked.

'Well, as a matter of fact,' Faulkner said, with a wry look, 'it was through a kind deed that he got to know *me*. He sent a very generous contribution to a cause with which I'm closely associated – the welfare of merchant seamen's dependents.' He smiled – an old man's deprecating smile. 'You might not think it now, Mr Mellanby, but I spent my life in the merchant service, and I was a liner captain when I retired . . . Anyhow, we put one of our usual appeals in *The Times,* and Roscoe sent a quite substantial cheque and a most friendly letter. I was very grateful, and asked him to come round for a drink and a chat – and I have to admit that I took to him.'

Mellanby nodded. 'He can be very charming and persuasive when he feels like it.'

'That's what I found. Also, we had some small interests in common. He told me he was in business in the Midlands – running, he said, a fleet of pleasure boats on the less active canals. He was most enthusiastic about canals – he thought they had quite a future, and that people would eventually use them for holidays as they now use the Broads. All that was needed, he said, was more capital to build the boats . . .' Faulkner sighed. 'I suppose I was very foolish, but I had no reason to doubt his good faith. He seemed a very prosperous young man, as well as most likeable. I asked him to stay with me while he was in London – I'm an old bachelor, living quite alone, and I was glad to have him. I trusted him completely. Actually, it was I who suggested that I should invest some money in his business. I'm not a rich man, but I'd saved a fair amount and I was interested. Damn it, I even pressed him! In the end he accepted a cheque for seven thousand pounds, and shortly afterwards he left for the West Country to buy, as he said, some additional craft.'

'And nothing else happened, I suppose,' Mellanby said.

'Not for some time – he did write to me once from Stourport, but after that there was a long silence. I began to get worried – he'd promised to send me share certificates in his company, but nothing came. Then I had some other financial troubles – the bottom suddenly fell out of some shares I owned in a company with Middle East connections, because of a political upset there – and I badly needed that seven thousand pounds or its equivalent . . . I was about to start making inquiries when I got another letter from him, from Bath, saying he hoped to send me the certificates soon . . . But it was a very vague letter.'

'He was playing for time, of course.'

'That was what *I* decided ... By now – very reluctantly – I'd begun to doubt his genuineness. I wrote back, rather stiffly, telling him I'd been forced to change my plans and asking him if he would be good enough to return the money, or some negotiable equivalent, at once ...'

Mellanby nodded. 'It was a letter that worried him a great deal.'

'I can well believe it ...' Faulkner sighed again. 'Well, I didn't do anything more about it during the next day or two – I was visiting some friends in Brighton. I hoped the cheque would be here when I got back. But it wasn't – there was nothing. Not even an acknowledgement or an explanation. Not even an excuse. So then I wrote the letter which you saw. I don't know what your own experience has been, Mr Mellanby, but I've no longer any doubts at all about Roscoe – and I think it would be much better if I put the matter in the hands of the police. Roscoe is not only a fraud – in my opinion he is not a redeemable character.'

'I agree with you about that,' Mellanby said. 'I'm certainly not expecting to redeem him. When he showed me your letter this morning, and asked me to help him, he had the effrontery practically to admit that he was a confidence man – trading, of course, on the fact that I owed him such a deep debt of gratitude. So I've no illusions about him at all. He's told me a pack of lies about himself, just as he did you – a different story, but for the same end. He's obviously quite unscrupulous ... But the fact remains that he did me the greatest service one man can do for another – risking, as I say, his own life – and it seems to me the only way I can repay him is to save him – on this occasion, at least – from going to jail. Indeed, I'm committed – I promised him, before he left, that I'd settle his account for him.'

'He's gone, has he?'

'Yes, I made it a condition that he should leave at once, and he cleared off after breakfast. I don't know where he's gone to, and frankly I don't care. It's all been a most distressing business ... What I do know, Mr Faulkner, is that you'll be doing me a service by accepting my cheque and not pressing any charge against him. Then I can forget all about it.'

94

'Well, I'm very reluctant' Faulkner said slowly. 'Mind you, I need the money, I'm not pretending I don't and I certainly shan't get it any other way . . . But I'm very reluctant indeed.'

'You feel he should be punished?'

'I think the scoundrel should be keel-hauled, Mr Mellanby!'

'Yet in your letter,' Mellanby said, 'you seemed to indicate that if he paid the money back you wouldn't pursue the matter.'

'If he'd paid it back of his own accord – or even a part of it – that at least would have been some sign of grace.'

'Try to see it from my point of view,' Mellanby said. 'Whatever his faults, he's an unusually brave man. Heroism like his must count for a lot. Particularly, I would think, with you . . . A mitigating factor, surely?'

'Well, yes . . . But leaving that aside, it seems to me most unjust that you should have to pay this large amount . . . Forgive me for asking, Mr Mellanby, but can you really afford it?'

'I can well afford it,' Mellanby said.

'I see . . . Well, you put me in a quandary. As I say, I need the money – but to accept such a large sum from a complete stranger . . .'

'I'm asking it as a favour,' Mellanby said.

'Well, of course, if you put it like that . . . It will certainly be a very great refief to me.'

Mellanby took out his cheque book with an inward sigh of thankfulness. Faulkner's relief would be nothing to his! 'It's all a question of what one's prepared to pay for peace of mind, Mr Faulkner,' he said. 'I know very well that if you brought a charge against Roscoe, and he was jailed – however much he deserves it – I should lie awake at night thinking how he'd pulled my wife and boy out of the sea, and how I could have saved him from prison if I'd tried a bit harder . . . So here's the cheque, and I'm grateful to you for taking it.'

'Well – thank you,' the old man said. 'It lifts a great weight from my mind . . . If you'll permit me to say so, I think your action is a most generous one . . .' – he gave a wintry smile – '. . . even if it is quite misguided!' He held out his knuckly hand. 'Let us hope that neither of us is troubled by Frank Roscoe again.'

Mellanby's smile was even more wintry. He had never disliked himself more than he did at that moment. 'Somehow,' he said, 'I don't think we shall be.'

Chapter Twenty-Two

With the settlement of Roscoe's debt, the danger of police inquiries seemed finally to have passed. Even Mellanby could see no further cause for anxiety on that score. A brief note of reiterated thanks and good wishes which arrived from Charles Faulkner the following afternoon was clearly intended to close the episode. It was possible, of course, that the old man would tell his friends about Mellanby's remarkable gesture – just possible. But even if he did, it wouldn't matter. The gesture, though extravagant, had been natural enough in the circumstances, and on its own it certainly wouldn't arouse the slightest suspicion. It was a pity, Mellanby thought, that he'd had to tell Faulkner that Roscoe had left after breakfast rather than the evening before, since that statement clashed with what he and Sally had put about in Bath – but as the contents of the morning letter had been the cause of his visit to London, he'd had no choice, In any case, the discrepancy wasn't likely to be found out. It was an untidiness, that was all.

Sally's relief was immeasurable. She felt a deep and almost humble gratitude to her husband, who had played a part he must have detested. She was secretly a little surprised at the resourceful, man-of-action way in which he'd handled the situation. Danger seemed to be bringing out new and unexpected qualities in him. It wasn't until the crisis was plainly over that she referred to the financial aspect – and then only tentatively. In strict fairness, she said, ought not George to pay a share of the seven thousand pounds? – especially as he could well afford it ... Probably he'd be glad to. But Mellanby was strongly against asking him, even if the chance occurred. No doubt he'd tell him what had happened, he said, if they ever met again, but the last thing he wanted at the moment was the transfer of a large sum of money from George to himself, which would be a difficult thing to account for if anyone started asking questions. Much better, he said, to leave well alone – particularly as they weren't in need of the money ... Sally was easily persuaded.

For a day or two, Mellanby continued to feel a slight uneasiness when he picked up the daily post. There was always the chance that Roscoe had left some unpaid bills in the town, or involved himself in some way that Mellanby didn't know about. Anything like that would mean more explanations, more subterfuge. But his fears proved groundless. No more letters came, and there were no more telephone inquiries. No one even mentioned Roscoe any more. In Bath, he was a forgotten man – and soon the trail would be cold.

Chapter Twenty-Three

There was still a reckoning, though, as Mellanby had always known there would be in the end – the reckoning in his own mind. He had been too numbed with shock at first, too busy grappling with deadly dangers later, to allow of much brooding. Now the shock was past the dangers over, and there was no longer any escape from himself and his memories . . . From the *real* truth . . .

He did his best to curb his thoughts. He argued the case through with himself, over and over, stressing everything he could find in his favour. Determinedly, he tried to take a sensible and balanced view of his deception. On every practical ground, he told himself, Sally and Sherston had been right. He'd done the best, the only rational thing, by agreeing to keep quiet. The proof was all around him. The family was safe. The children were happy – they would never know. Sense and logic approved of what he'd done. In the daytime, sense and logic almost prevailed. Sitting in his study, with his work before him, and Sally close at hand, and an air of security all around him, he could, with a great effort of will, put Roscoe from his mind. Busying himself in town with societies and causes, talking with his friends and colleagues, he could force himself to concentrate . . . . But sense and logic couldn't give him tranquil nights. Will power applied in the wakeful early hours merely left him drained. As the days passed, he found it more and more difficult to get any real rest. The moment he lay down, thoughts of the quarry filled his mind – morbid, ghastly thoughts. The picture of Roscoe's body rotting in its grave obsessed him. *His* handiwork! For the first time in his life he began to take sleeping tablets – but his brain fought them, so that they always worked too late to do him any good. He began to lose weight that he could ill spare; his face became gaunt. It was as though his inner struggle were consuming him.

Sally watched him with growing distress and alarm. She had always known that it would be hard for him to forget, but she had never foreseen anything like this. Desperately, achingly, she tried to think of some new way to help him. Everything that devoted love could do, she had already done. Discussion seemed to have reached a dead end. She had tried several times to go over things with him again, to lift him out of his morbidity, but she seemed to have lost all power of persuasion. Sometimes she felt that she had even lost contact with him. It was something new in their married life, and it added sharply to her unhappiness. Perhaps, she thought things would be better if they could get away together. A holiday might do him good – a complete change, a cruise, perhaps, after the children were back at school. Evelyn would probably take care of them for a week or two . . . Yet Mellanby seemed so tortured and hag-ridden that she doubted if anything but time would make much difference.

One afternoon – it was nearly a fortnight after Roscoe's death – she went into the study with a letter for him. He was leaning on the desk with his head in his hands, motionless. At the sound of her entry he jerked upright and guiltily turned the page of the book that lay open in front of him. Sally put the letter down, then drew up a chair beside him.

'Darling – we can't go on like this.'

'We've no choice,' he said.

'But, John, you're going to make yourself really ill.'

'Well, you don't imagine I'm doing it on purpose . . .?' He saw the look of distress in her face, and put a hand on hers in swift contrition. 'I'm sorry . . . I'm ashamed of myself, Sally. I'm a damned weakling, I know that. I despise myself for not being able to forget it. But I can't – I *can't*!'

'*Darling!* – oh, if only I could help you. If only I could understand *why* it preys on your mind so – *why* you can't forget . . . Why should it be so much worse for you than for me? – after all, I urged you on. Or for George? – I'm quite certain he's not making himself ill over it.'

'People are made differently.'

'I wouldn't have said I was made so differently – I'd have thought I had a normal amount of conscience. But I certainly don't see this as you do . . . Look, darling, I know we've been over it again and again, but I have to keep on saying it – all you did was hit a man twice your size who was wrecking your home and threatening your children – and actually beating George into a pulp . . .'

'And I killed him.'

'It was an accident. You didn't even hit him very hard – and anyway I'm not at all sure it was the chair that hit his head. It didn't look like it to me – he dodged and *I* think it was his shoulder that you hit. I think he fell and banged his head on the fireplace and that was sheer bad luck. Why blame yourself? Heavens, it's not as though you meant to kill him.'

'I *wanted* to kill him,' Mellanby said.

Sally gave him a startled look. 'Darling, that's nonsense . . . You probably hated him at that moment – who wouldn't have done? – but not in that way . . . You, of all people . . .!'

'I tell you I wanted to kill him,' Mellanby repeated. 'And not out of hate. You don't understand, Sally. I was frightened of him. *Terrified!* When I picked up that chair and went for him it wasn't just in anger, or to help George, as it would have been with most men. I did it out of fear – sheer, naked, uncontrolled fear. Fear of his strength and his viciousness, and his razor threats, and of all the things he might do. I'd only one thought in my mind at that moment and it was to smash him down, crush him, get rid of him, *finish* him – just as though he'd been a dangerous snake. God knows it was a pretty puny effort and with ordinary luck he'd scarcely have felt it – but that's beside the point. If ever a man had murder in his heart, I had at that moment . . .'

'At that moment, perhaps – it's not surprising . . .' Sally was pale.

'If you hit a man with murder in your heart, and he dies, that *is* murder . . .'

'It was he who made you afraid.'

'It was I who hadn't the guts to keep control of myself . . . I know what I felt, Sally, and I know what I did. I dare say there are lots of people who wouldn't worry about it at all, who'd think it was all justified. I wish to God I were one of them – but I'm not. I'm ashamed. I've got a damned conscience gnawing at me day and night, tearing me to shreds . . . Oh, *Sally!*'

She put her arms round him. 'Darling, you've nothing to be ashamed of – nothing at all . . . You're not being fair to yourself. You've got more real courage than anyone I ever met . . . John, whatever you felt at the time, he brought it all on himself – every bit of it . . . It was *all* his fault . . .'

'He started it, I know. I can argue the case as well as you. But it doesn't alter the fact that I'm going to be haunted for the rest of my life by a feeling of guilt and a squalid secret.'

As she looked at his strained, suffering face, Sally suddenly realized how illusory was the security she had struggled to preserve. She had been so confident they had chosen the right course – so unimaginatively sure. Now, for the first time, she had doubts. What, after all, was John's physical freedom going to be worth to him, if his peace of mind were shattered? What was it going to be worth to her, watching his torment? What ultimate happiness could there be for the children in a haunted home? And yet . . .

For a while she sat in anguished silence, scarcely daring to frame the question that was in her mind. Then she forced the words out. 'John – do you still want to confess?'

He didn't reply at once. When he did, it was with an emphasis that surprised her. 'No – that's impossible now.'

'If you do, darling, I – I won't try to stop you . . . It would be dreadful – but anything's better than seeing you like this.'

He shook his head. 'After all that's happened, it's quite unthinkable . . . I'm committed . . . Apart from anything else, I gave George my word that I'd see it through, and I can't go back on that . . . It's something I've ruled right out.'

'You're sure . . .?'

'Quite sure . . . I wasn't leading up to that, Sally, when I started to talk – or anything like it. I didn't even mean to tell you what was worrying me so much. It just came out. I know perfectly well that I've got to put up with it – we both have . . . Anyhow, perhaps things will seem better now that I've got it off my chest. At least I've confessed to you!'

'Yes, darling,' Sally said. 'If only I could give you absolution!'

Chapter Twenty-Four

As it turned out things did improve – for a day or two. Mellanby, having shared his burden, seemed much less oppressed, and slept soundly for the first time since Roscoe's death. Sally began to hope that the worst was over, and that in the end things might even return to normal. Then, out of a clear sky, a new crisis burst upon them like a thunderclap – and this time – there was no simple way out.

It was one evening after dinner. Kira had gone out for a short walk. Sally and Mellanby were drinking coffee, reading the papers, and occasionally exchanging comments about the news. Sally had the *Daily Mail;* Mellanby, pipe in mouth, was browsing through the local paper, the *Bath Gazette*. It was a peaceful and pleasantly domestic scene.

Then a headline caught Mellanby's eye. He read down the paragraph, frowning a little. Suddenly he gave a gasp of horror.

The item read:

BLACKETT'S LANE BY-PASS
Ready By Easter?

It is learned on good authority that plans to divert the main Bath–Radbury road through Blackett's Lane and by-pass the village of Eversleigh are to be advanced by several months. The decision to expedite the work has been taken following renewed protests by Eversleigh residents over the mounting toll of accidents in the narrow village street. Some preliminary work in the lane, including the widening of a bridge, has already been done, and it is now hoped to complete the whole scheme by Easter. The lane, in its new form, will be thirty feet wide and, like the main road, will have a cycle track on one side and a footpath on the other. The *Gazette* understands that Blackett's Lane will be closed to all traffic from September 15th until its re-opening as a by-pass next year.

Chapter Twenty-Five

'They'll find him, of course,' Mellanby said.

Sally finished reading the paragraph and slowly put the paper down. Her face was ashen. 'They might not, John ... How deep do they dig when they make a road?'

'I don't know – I expect it varies ... But deep enough!'

'More than four feet?'

'At least five or six, I should think, in a case like this perhaps more ... A main road to take heavy traffic would have to have tremendous foundations.'

'Perhaps they'll add all the width on the other side – away from the quarry.'

Mellanby shook his head. 'For a thirty foot road and two paths they'll tear the whole place up ... They're *bound* to find him. The body's so close to the verge, there isn't a chance.'

'It was madness to put it there,' Sally burst out.

'George said it was the only place soft enough to dig and naturally *he* wouldn't think of the lane being widened ... We ought to have done, though – we knew about it...' Mellanby gazed fixedly at his wife. 'Sally ... we're in a frightful mess.'

There was a short, desperate silence. Then Sally said, 'John – I know it's horrible – but do you think they'll still be able to identify him?'

'I expect they will – they have all sorts of ways ... And they'll find the suitcase, with all his things in it ... They'll check up on the laundry marks ...'

'Some of them are *our* laundry marks!' Sally said.

'Yes ... They'll have no difficulty at all. They'll find out who he was, and they'll come straight to us. They'll learn about the caravan being in the quarry and about our association with the Sherstons. The medical report will probably say that Roscoe died about that time, so they'll be more than suspicious. They'll ask all those questions we decided we couldn't answer – and a lot more besides. They'll find out about the cheque I paid to Faulkner, and they'll talk to him, and they'll discover I lied about when Roscoe left here . . . They'll discover everything. It'll be the end of us . . .' Mellanby got up and began to pace about the room. Slowly his expression hardened, '*If* they find the body.'

Sally stared at him. 'But I thought you said . . .'

'Sally, I'm in this thing up to my neck – almost literally! The situation can't get any worse. We were probably wrong to try to hush things up, but we made the decision and now we've got to go through with it. There's no road back – and I'm not going to give in . . . I'm going to dig Roscoe up and bury him somewhere else!'

'John!'

'I know . . .! It's unspeakable. The mere thought turns my stomach. Well, it'll just have to turn . . .! I'm going to do it, Sally. It's the only way.'

Sally sat frozen with horror. Her whole being revolted at the prospect – it was worse than anything she'd ever imagined . . . There *must* be some alternative. But, try as she might, she could think of none.

'Yes – I suppose it *is* the only way . . .' she said at last. 'But, John, oughtn't we to try to find George, first? He ought to help – and it would make it easier for you.'

'It would, I agree – but how would we start? We haven't the faintest idea where he is.'

'Perhaps we could get the AA to look for him . . . You'd have to think of some reason why you needed him urgently, that's all.'

Mellanby considered for a moment, then shook his head. 'I don't think we can afford to wait for George – if he's camping in a quiet spot like the quarry it might take ages to find him. We just haven't the time. If Blackett's Lane is going to be closed on the 15th, that only gives us ten days at the most – and the workmen will probably start moving in well before that . . . The only safe way is for us to rely on ourselves – and we'll have to move fast. I think we ought to do it at once.'

'You don't mean – *tonight?*'

'Well, no, there'll be too much planning for that . . . I'll have to do some reconnoitring – find a suitable place. There'll be preparations, too – equipment to think about . . .' He broke off. 'I'm afraid I shall need quite a bit of help from you, Sally.'

'Of course,' Sally said.

'I'll spare you all I can . . .'

'I know you will.'

'I suggest we make a start tomorrow night, then. It'll take us two nights to finish, at least – one to move the body, and one to move the suitcase. Perhaps more – there'll be all the filling in, as well as the digging. We'll move the suitcase first – get acclimatized . . .!'

Sally looked at him, startled. This was a Mellanby she didn't recognize. 'Darling – are you all right?'

'I'm fine,' he said. 'I've just about got to the point where I don't give a damn, that's all.'

Chapter Twenty-Six

Early next morning Mellanby drove alone to Blackett's Lane. Except for the now-completed bridge there were no signs at all that it was soon to become a busy thoroughfare. There were distant farming noises from, the fields, but the lane itself was deserted. Mellanby drove straight to the quarry and parked his car. Then he crossed to the burial site in the bushes, firmly closing his mind to all but the practical aspects of his task. It took him a little time to find the spot where Sherston had buried the suitcase, but as he pushed the light covering of leaves aside with the iron ferrule of his stick, his experienced eye at last picked out the tell-tale traces of disturbance – a slight upward bulge, an unfilled crack, the faint impression of a heel. The place was three or four yards from Roscoe's grave. Mellanby marked its centre with a large stone, so that he would be able to find it more easily at night. Then he started to prospect around for an alternative site.

The quarry floor itself, as George had said, offered no possibilities at all. Mellanby chose a low point in the rough-hewn stone cliff and climbed to the top to see what lay behind the quarry. He found himself at the edge of a large field of stubble, with stooks of recently-cut corn dotted over it. At the far end of the field a group of farm workers were busily loading the corn into carts. No good at all, he decided. Any disturbance of the even stubble would be conspicuous, and people would be around clearing the field for some time yet In any case, a steep bank from the road made it awkward to get at. The new site must be as easy to reach, and as close to the old one, as possible ...

Mellanby lowered himself cautiously down the bank. He was

just going to step into the road when he caught a faint hum, the sound of approaching tyres, and dropped down into the undergrowth. A moment later a man sped by on a bicycle, pedalling fast. Slightly shaken, Mellanby watched him out of sight. Then he crossed to the other side of the lane. The prospects were much better there. Behind a thin hedge of hazel and bramble he found a field which looked as though it had been abandoned after an unsuccessful attempt at cultivation. The marks of the plough were still there, but bracken and heather were beginning to take over and the place would soon revert to heath. A rusty wire fence had wide gaps in it making access easy. Mellanby passed through a gap and walked slowly up and down, parallel with the road but about twenty yards from it, examining the ground and prodding it with his stick. The soil was dry and peaty – it should be fairly easy to dig. Near the lane an eroded hollow with a vertical edge showed that it had adequate depth. The site was a bit exposed, especially to the field above the quarry, but at night that wouldn't matter. Mellanby decided he need look no further. He found another stone and marked a spot well back from the road and almost opposite the gap he'd come through. Satisfied, he returned to the car.

Back at the house, he reported the results of his reconnaissance to Sally, and they discussed further arrangements. It would be unwise – and unfair, they agreed – for them to go out secretly at night without telling Kira – she might hear the car, and wake and worry. It would be better, Sally suggested, if they said they were going to dine out and go on to friends afterwards, and might be back late. The Blakes in Bristol would probably have them for coffee, if she rang them. Mellanby agreed. For the second night, they would have to think of something else – but that could wait Sally went off to tell Kira, and Mellanby retired to the garage to make his own preparations. Most of the things he would need for the night's work were in an adjoining tool shed, put there after his last 'dig' – an entrenching tool and spade, gum boots, boiler suit, and electric hand lamp. He tested the battery, found it in good order, and stowed the things away in the car boot. Then he stood frowning for a moment. He'd need something to drink – but it wouldn't be safe for Sally to try to smuggle a flask of coffee out. He'd have to make do with water. He found a clean bottle and filled it at the garden tap. Anything else? There was a folded tarpaulin which he sometimes used to cover small excavations in wet weather – better put that in the car as well. He wouldn't need it tonight, but he'd probably need it the next night for – he forced his mind to frame the ghastly word – for the remains.

Now there was nothing to do but wait. Sally occupied herself with the children, the best of all distractions. Mellanby walked a little, and read a little, but found it impossible to settle to anything for long. There must surely come a time, he thought, when the sort of tension they were constantly living under became a norm, a habit and the brain went numb – but that time certainly hadn't come yet. Through every moment of every dragging hour, he was acutely conscious of the task ahead – and of its dangers.

The first spell of waiting ended at six. Sally gave Kira a few final instructions and they said goodbye to the children. Then they drove to Bristol, where they lingered over a meal that almost choked them. At nine they called on their friends the Blakes and took coffee with them, forcing themselves to make light conversation. At ten-thirty they set off thankfully for Blackett's Lane. The weather forecast on the radio that evening had been 'changeable,' but the night looked like being dry and warm. The moon wouldn't be up till nearly one in the morning. Conditions were perfect for their enterprise.

It was a little after eleven when they reached the lane. Driving along it Mellanby kept an eye open for possible parked cars, but the place seemed quite deserted. Once in the quarry, with the Humber's lights off, he felt reasonably secure. They could begin at once.

They had been carefully over the drill, and knew just what to do. Sally, subdued but determined, took up a position in the lane a few yards from where Mellanby would be digging. The moment she saw or heard anything, she would join him, and he would douse his light and wait till the danger had passed. Mellanby had already donned his boiler suit and gum boots and brought the tools over to the bushes. He quickly found his marker, hung the electric lamp on a branch so that its diffused light was thrown downwards to the ground – and started to dig.

It was heavy work, and he was soon sweating freely. The need for speed was in his mind all the time and he toiled without resting. The soil, though recently disturbed, had been closely compacted by George's heavy tread, and it had to be hewn out in great lumps. It was nearly half an hour before Mellanby's spade struck the resilient top of the suitcase, more than four feet down. It took him another half hour to free the case, for he had to open up a much larger hole before he had elbow room to get at it. But at last it was out, and he stood back with a grunt of satisfaction, mopping his face.

'All right?' Sally called. It was almost the first word she'd spoken for an hour.

'Yes, I've got it . . . I'm going to fill in now.'

Filling was easier, but it had to be done with care. As long as the body was still buried close by, there must be no obvious signs of digging anywhere. Mellanby shovelled and stamped, scraping in the last of the loose soil. When the ground was level he swept leaves over it again and drew the brambles across and obliterated his footmarks by the light of the lamp. Then he picked up the damp suitcase and the tools and joined Sally. The time was just after half past twelve.

Sally looked at him anxiously. His hair was matted, his face streaked and filthy. 'Darling, you're soaking . . . Oh, I do wish I could do more to help.'

'You're doing fine,' Mellanby told her. 'Don't worry – I'm an old hand at this . . .'

His cheerfulness didn't deceive her. 'I've got the water here,' she said. 'Would you like some?'

'Please.' He took the bottle and gulped down several mouthfuls. 'That's better . . .' He handed it back. 'Well, I suppose we ought to get on – I'll feel a lot happier when this load of dynamite is underground again.'

Together they carried the case and took and lamp to the new

marker. There was no cover now from any bushes and Mellanby told Sally to keep an especially careful look-out. She returned to the lane and mounted guard again and once more Mellanby started to dig. He would need to hack out a trench about five feet long by three wide to get the necessary depth. A sliver of moon was just beginning to show above the trees, and he knew he had to hurry. For fifteen minutes he dug without a pause. His muscles were aching now. His hands were blistered ... That wouldn't do, he thought – someone might notice. Tomorrow he must wear gloves ... Tomorrow! This was bad enough, but tomorrow would be infinitely worse ... Still, they were making progress. No point in dwelling on horrors to come ... He toiled on.

Suddenly there was a sharp call from Sally in the lane – 'John – what's that light?' He looked up, startled. There was a bright glow in the sky behind the quarry – it seemed to be coming from the field. In a moment two parallel beams of light stabbed the darkness. They were swinging like searchlights towards him. He dropped his spade and flung himself down beside the hole, pressing himself against the ground. The beam swept over him and turned away. It was a car up in the cornfield! He could hear its engine now. There seemed to be a positive blaze of light up there. More than one car, surely? What the hell were they up to? Suddenly a tractor engine sprang to life – and at once he knew what was happening. He got cautiously to his feet and stood there for a moment, uncertain what to do. Then he went over to Sally.

'What on earth's going on?' she asked in a frightened voice.

'They're going to get the rest of the corn in,' Mellanby said. 'Using car lights and moonlight ... They often do it when they think the weather's going to break ...'

Sally gave a little gasp. 'Of course ...! I couldn't imagine what it was ... Darling, how far have you got?'

'I ought to go down another two feet.'

'Do you think they can see you from the field?'

'Not if the lights aren't shining on me, but it's very unnerving when they swing across ... In the beam, they probably could ... Perhaps they'll settle down in a few minutes ...'

They waited. The cars were still manoeuvring about, taking up their positions round the field. Distant voices came floating over the quarry towards them. Someone was shouting instructions . . . Then the headlamps grew steady. The note of the tractor engine changed. It was on the move. Work must have started . . .

'I'll have to risk it,' Mellanby said tensely. 'They'll be here all night . . .'

Sally nodded. 'Do be careful!' she called after him, as he slipped away.

Back in the field, he redoubled his efforts. With the moon up, and the lights glowing above the quarry, he could see well enough now without the lamp. He hacked and shovelled, with one eye all the time on the skyline. He had dug out another foot of earth before the next alarm. Then the noise of the tractor suddenly grew louder. It was coming nearer. It must be hauling its first load. Moving towards some gate. Its headlamps were swinging . . . Mellanby dropped flat again, his heart pounding. The beam was almost on him. It *was* on him. For a second, it seemed to hold him in a white glare. They'd seen him! They'd send someone down – it was all over . . . Then the spotlight passed. The tractor went on its way. Mellanby got slowly to his feet. He felt badly shaken. He couldn't go on like this – it was too dangerous . . . Better to fill in the hole and take a chance on the depth. At least the suitcase would be out of reach of any ploughshare, if the field should be cultivated again . . . Quickly, he levelled the bottom of the hole and lowered the suitcase in and flung back the soil stamping down each layer. The earth wouldn't all go in and he had to carry large lumps to the edge of the field and scatter them amongst the hazels. When the hole was full and firm he put back the turf he'd cut from the top and stamped that down too. In a few days, with luck, the surface would look much like the rest of the field. Kneeling down, so that his body shielded the lamp, he flashed the light on for a second to make sure that everything was all right. Then he gathered up the tools and walked heavily over to Sally. The tractor was just coming back into the cornfield.

'Well, I think that's done the trick,' he said wearily.

'Darling – you were marvellous . . .'

'It was a pretty near thing, that tractor light . . .'

'I know . . . Come on, let's get you home.'

In silence, they crossed the quarry floor to the car. Mellanby stripped off his boiler suit and gum boots and locked everything up in the back. Then he slumped down in the passenger seat Sally took the wheel. Neither of them spoke much on the way home. Mellanby was too tired to talk. Sally was too worried. Tonight had been nerve-racking enough the prospect of another night like it, only worse, weighed like lead . . .

As they neared the house, Sally began to wonder if Kira would wake. If she did, they would have to say they had had a breakdown . . . John, with the marks of his digging still on him, would have to keep out of the way . . . Very quietly, she turned the car into the drive with the headlamps off and let it trickle to a stop. There was no sound from the house. They entered with the stealth of burglars. No one called out. Evidently they were going to be all right. Mellanby went straight upstairs to clean himself up in the bathroom. By the time Sally joined him, he was getting into bed. Five minutes after that he was asleep.

Chapter Twenty-Seven

It was after nine in the morning when Mellanby was roused by Sally's voice and the clink of a cup. He heaved himself up on one elbow, stiffly. Sally was sitting in her dressing gown, pouring tea at the little table between their beds.

'Hallo darling,' she said. She gave him an affectionate though rather wan smile. 'Well – do you feel better for your six hours solid?'

'I ache a lot more!' he said. He took the cup she handed to him, and gratefully sipped the hot tea. 'Have you seen Kira and the kids?'

'Yes . . .'

'Any comments?'

'They hoped we had a lovely time . . .! Kira didn't hear us come in – so everything seems to be under control so far.'

'That's a relief . . . Did you sleep all right?'

'Not really – it took me ages to get off . . .' Sally gave him an odd look. 'As a matter of fact, darling, I'd no sooner closed my eyes than I had the most extraordinary thought . . . I've been longing for you to wake up so that I could tell you . . .'

'Well, I'm awake now – just about!'

'John – you remember when George rang you up that night to tell you that Roscoe had died . . .?'

'Yes . . .'

'What did he say? – about finding Roscoe. I expect you told me, but I've forgotten the details.'

Mellanby frowned in thought. 'Well – as far as I can recall, he said he'd been out for a short stroll, and Roscoe had seemed all right when he'd left, and when he'd got back he was dead.'

'Did he say when it happened? – finding him, I mean.'

'Yes – he said about half an hour before he rang me.'

'That's what I thought . . . And how long after the phone call was it before you reached the caravan?'

'Oh, – about three quarters of an hour . . . What's all this leading up to, Sally?'

'John, do you realize that not counting interruptions, it took you nearly two hours to dig out that new hole last night working at top speed?'

Mellanby stared at her. 'Well . . .?'

'Well, that was the thought that kept me awake . . . Darling, if George was telling us the truth he'd have had less than an hour and a half to dig a much bigger hole – a full-sized grave – and get Roscoe's body into it and start filling it in again, before you got there . . . Could he have done it?'

A look of puzzlement settled on Mellanby's face. The point hadn't occurred to him before – he'd been much too upset on the night of Roscoe's death, and much too preoccupied with danger since, to think about it – but he hadn't much doubt of the answer now. He'd done enough field work in his life to know the sort of timetable that digging involved. Slowly, he shook his head. 'No, I don't think he could,' he said.

'He's very strong, of course . . .'

'Even so, I can't see him doing it . . . It would have taken him quite a while to find a suitable place . . . Then he had to go and phone me, and get back . . . And he was digging in a tougher spot than I was, with only a spade . . .' Mellanby shook his head again. 'I'd say it was absolutely impossible . . . Sally, this is fantastic . . .!'

'It is, isn't it . . .? If we're right, it means that Roscoe must have died before George said he did, and George must have got on with the digging and not told you about the death until the grave was almost finished!'

'That seems incredible . . .'

'I don't know . . . He was obviously determined the body should be buried, and he didn't know whether you'd agree or not ... He might well have gone ahead on his own.'

'It would have been a shocking thing to do,' Mellanby said 'Heavens, it was bad enough to go as far as he did without consultation – but to keep the death a secret deliberately, so that he could present me with an accomplished fact ...! Sally, that would be unforgivable ... I simply can't believe it.'

'What other explanation can there be?'

'But it doesn't make sense ... After all, he didn't *know* what my attitude would be – I might just as easily have turned to and helped him dig ... It certainly wouldn't be the natural thing to do. If a man dies, and someone besides yourself is jointly to blame, the first thing you do, surely, is to get in touch ...? You'd be anxious to consult – you'd want to share the responsibility ... I can understand George going ahead and using up the time before I arrived – but not keeping back the truth as a calculated policy. I can't imagine anyone doing that in the circumstances.'

There was a little silence. Then Sally said, 'Well, darling, facts are facts, aren't they? If what you say about the digging is right, that's what *must* have happened ... Unless, of course, you're prepared to consider an even worse alternative.'

'What do you mean?'

'Isn't it obvious? If Roscoe died when George said he did, and it took George more than an hour and a half to dig the grave, then George must have started digging it when Roscoe was still alive!'

Chapter Twenty-Eight

Mellanby said, 'What a horrible suggestion . . .!' He looked appalled. 'That can be ruled out right away.'

'Can it?' Sally's face was wooden.

'Of course it can . . . If George had had the slightest suspicion that Roscoe might die, he'd have called a doctor straight away – not dug a grave! George isn't a monster.'

'I'm beginning to wonder,' Sally said. 'We don't really know George very well, do we? We don't know what he's capable of.'

'We know him well enough for that, I should think.' Mellanby gazed at her incredulously. 'Why, it would have been deliberate murder – just as much as if George had gone in to Roscoe and hit him with a spanner.'

There was a little pause. Then Sally said, 'Perhaps he did just that!'

'*Sally* . . .! You haven't any right . . .'

'I've as much right as George had to keep the truth from you,' Sally said stubbornly.

'You haven't the right to fling frightful accusations like that around . . .'

'Darling, I've been thinking about this for hours – I'm not just talking wildly . . . Look, you said yourself that digging the grave without telling you about the death wasn't natural – and I agree. If George had merely been concerned with the safety of both of you, he'd have phoned you first – so that isn't the explanation . . . If he'd suspected that Roscoe might die, and hadn't had anything more on his conscience than what happened at this house, he'd have called a doctor right away, if only for his own sake – anybody would ... So that isn't the explanation, either ... But if he'd deliberately finished Roscoe off himself, then that *would* account for his not phoning you, and for his frantic haste to get the body buried ... Don't you realize? – there'd have been marks on the body he wouldn't want you to see!'

For a moment, there was an uneasy silence. Then Mellanby said, 'Well, you have a point there, I suppose ... But there's not a scrap of evidence to support it.'

'Isn't there ...? Didn't George keep on saying that Roscoe wasn't fit to live – even after the fight was over and Roscoe couldn't do any more harm?'

'That's a very different thing from killing him.'

'Well, *I* think he meant it ... He hated Roscoe much more than you did, you know, and in a far more violent way. There really was murder in *his* heart when he came here – he was absolutely beside himself. And I certainly don't see him as a forgiving type. We don't know much about him, but there's one thing we do know – his feelings about Eve were primitive and he'd had a rough upbringing. He's just the sort who would try to take his revenge. And think how easy it would have seemed, John, with Roscoe lying there only half recovered, and a convenient place outside to bury him, and no one but ourselves knowing what had happened or where he was ... And there was almost no risk – George would know you'd have to cooperate with him afterwards, because you thought you were in it too.'

'I *was* in it,' Mellanby said. 'It was I who hit him. All this is pure imagination ...'

'I don't think it is – I'd say everything ties up. I think it's quite possible you've been blaming yourself all this time for something you never did ... A strong, tough man like Roscoe doesn't die from an ordinary bang on the head – and that fall of his wasn't really so terrific, you know ... Honestly, darling, did he *look* as though he was going to die, when George took him away? You know he didn't – he was already beginning to come round. You certainly thought he'd be all right – if it had occurred to you for a moment that he wouldn't be, you'd never have let him be taken away like that – you'd have insisted on a doctor at once. We were both absolutely staggered when we heard he was dead – and we had good reason to be!'

Mellanby still looked unconvinced. 'I can see what you're trying to do, Sally – and don't think I'm not grateful. You want to take the load off me, and God knows I'd be only too thankful if you could – but I'm afraid it's not going to work. The fact is, you've really thought all this up because you wanted to.'

'That's not true, John – not entirely, anyway . . . Surely you agree there's a case?'

'Oh, there's a sort of case, I suppose – but there's still not a scrap of real evidence to back it up . . . Anyhow, I just can't believe it. A lot of the things you said about George may be true, but I can't see him as a cold-blooded murderer deliberately finishing a helpless man. And that's not all . . . Aren't you overlooking something rather important?'

'What?'

'Why, Eve, of course . . . I thought you liked her a lot . . . Can you see *her* cooperating in a diabolical thing like this?'

'Eve took sleeping pills that night,' Sally said quietly. 'She wouldn't have known a thing about it.'

Chapter Twenty-Nine

Mellanby was silent over breakfast. He still considered Sally's idea fantastic, but he found it impossible to dismiss it from his mind. It was all very well, he realized, to say he couldn't imagine Sherston as a cold-blooded murderer – but wasn't that, perhaps, starting at the wrong end? Whatever Sherston's reasons had been, there was no doubt at all that he'd behaved in a pretty infamous way. At the best, he'd been guilty of a gross, an unpardonable deception. If he was capable of that, against all expectation, might he not be capable of far worse things? Could murder really be ruled out? Not, certainly, without more consideration. As soon as breakfast was over Mellanby took himself off for a walk to think things out.

Carefully and conscientiously, he went over in his mind the various points in Sally's case ... There were gaps, undoubtedly. There were weaknesses. People often did guilty seeming things for innocent reasons ... But not, surely, hustling a body secretly into a grave? What innocent reason could there possibly be for that – except the one they'd already discounted ...?

What about other aspects of Sherston's behaviour? What light did they throw? There was the message Sherston had asked Eve to pass on when she'd telephoned, saying that he was a bit worried about Roscoe ... Not much help there. A message showing some anxiety would have been necessary, of course, to prepare the way for the later announcement of the death, if that had been planned. But it could equally have been genuine ...

There were the contents of that message, though. Mellanby wondered again – *did* people with serious head injuries come round, and lapse back into unconsciousness, and then suddenly go out like a light? Didn't they more often sink into a deep coma and slowly fade away? He would have to ask someone who knew. If the symptoms Sherston had described proved to be unlikely, that would certainly be a point against him . . .

Mellanby's thoughts ranged . . . What about Sherston asking if Kira had been told of the night's happenings, when he'd rung up with news of the death? A point in his favour, surely? If he'd already killed Roscoe, hadn't he left that bit of checking up rather late? Would he have dared to risk murder without assuring himself about Kira beforehand . . .? Or had he taken it for granted that Sally wouldn't want to talk about it that night . . .? Had he, perhaps, even overlooked Kira altogether until the thing was done? That would account for his undoubted relief . . . But it didn't seem very likely . . .

There was one significant point, of course, that Sally hadn't even thought of. Sherston had been very willing indeed to take Roscoe to the caravan. Strangely willing, perhaps, after all that had happened. He'd actually suggested it . . . It might have been no more than the considerate action it had seemed – but it might have been the eager removal of an intended victim. On the whole, Mellanby thought, a point against Sherston . . .

Then there was the rather hurried way he'd cleared out of the district after the burial . . . Understandable enough that he'd wanted to leave, of course, but he could at least have said where he was going . . . And he could certainly have telephoned by now, as he'd promised to do. Why hadn't he . . .? Was there an element of flight in all this?

What about motive . . .? Revenge? – well, it was possible . . . Revenge and fear, mixed . . .? After all, Roscoe had twice made approaches to Eve, the second time with reckless violence . . . Had Sherston thought perhaps, that this formidable thug might try it yet again – and planned to kill him to make sure he didn't . . .? Or, of course, the act could have been done on a sudden impulse – an opportunity taken. Murder *would* have seemed very simple in that place . . . Mellanby's imagination could vividly conjure up the scene – Eve in a drugged sleep well before midnight; the lonely, silent quarry; the helpless man; the ease with which Roscoe's worthless life could have been ended. One crack with the spanner ... But had it happened?

Mellanby scarcely knew what to think now. He distrusted his own feelings – he was too aware of his desperate desire to shift the blame from himself. There was certainly a case – but was it stronger or weaker than before? He didn't know ... All he knew was that things couldn't be left as they were – that, somehow or other, the situation had got to be cleared up ... At the very least, he was entitled to an explanation of Sherston's behaviour ...

He turned for home, quickening his pace.

Chapter Thirty

Sally was with Kira and the children, picking Victoria plums at the bottom of the garden, when Mellanby reached the house. At the sound of his voice she detached herself and hurried up the path to meet him.

'Have you decided anything, darling . . .?' She studied his face anxiously.

'I think we must try to find the caravan,' Mellanby said.

She gave a little sigh of relief. 'Yes, I'm sure it's the thing to do . . .'

'You may be right or wrong about Sherston – I don't know – but one way or the other it should be possible to settle the matter . . . In any case, I want to see him.'

'I should think so . . .! Let's hope we're not too late, that's all.'

'What do you mean?'

'Well, it occurred to me – if George *was* responsible for Roscoe's death, he's hardly likely to have stayed in England. He may be hundreds of miles away on the Continent by now.'

'I rather doubt that,' Mellanby said. 'Not with the caravan, anyway – the ferry boats are always pretty well booked up at this time of year. Remember what a wait we had at Boulogne last summer? – and that was only a car. He'd be very fortunate to have got a place at such short notice.'

'Perhaps so . . .'

'Anyhow, we should be able to check that quite easily with the motoring organizations – there can't be so many caravans crossing.'

'Do you remember the number of George's car?'

'I've got it somewhere – I made a note of it when Roscoe was stuck in the lane with the caravan.'

'That's lucky . . .! John, what exactly will you say if we do find him? It's going to be rather awkward, isn't it?'

Mellanby looked grim. 'It could be very awkward, I should think . . .! We'll just have to take a step at a time.'

'Starting where?'

'Well, I'll begin by telling him about the crises we've had to face – Faulkner's letter, and now the road widening . . . They'll seem perfectly good reasons for going after him . . . I'll tell him about my digging last night, and what a time it took. Then I'll switch to his effort, and say I'm puzzled. He'll have to give some explanation . . . I must say I'll be most interested to hear what it is!'

'He'll probably give the reason we thought of first – that he wanted to get Roscoe buried before you had a chance to interfere. It's about all he can say.'

'If it doesn't happen to be the true reason,' Mellanby said, 'it may not occur to him right away. We may catch him completely off balance . . . He'll have Eve to think about, don't forget – assuming she knows nothing . . . He may be in quite a difficulty.'

'That's true . . .'

'Anyhow, we'll just have to see how things go . . . You might have a chance to take Eve aside and talk to her alone before we really get started – that might produce something useful . . . Did she ever give you her version of what happened that night?'

'Not in detail, no.'

'Well, we ought to try to get it . . . When did she wake up, I wonder, and what did Sherston tell her? Had he already phoned me? How far had he got with the grave? All that sort of thing . . . She might give a rather different account from the one Sherston gave, and any discrepancy would be interesting . . . With luck, you might pick up quite a bit of indirect evidence that way – always supposing there's anything to pick up . . . Or, of course, we might find it better to accuse Sherston directly if he seemed at all uneasy . . . Sort of shock tactics. Force him to talk.'

'You mean he might be made to admit it?'

'You never know – he might find it difficult to do anything else if he were in a sufficiently tight corner ... At least, the way he reacted would help us to make up our own minds about him. We could decide the next step after that.'

Sally nodded. There was a little silence. Then she said, 'Suppose you were convinced he'd done it, John – would you tell the police?'

'I think we'll face that problem when it arises,' Mellanby said, with the ghost of a smile. 'I'm very much afraid it never will ... Now I'd better get on to the motoring people about the caravan.'

Sally put a hand on his arm. 'Darling – what about tonight? Can't we leave it for a day or two, now, and see what happens?'

Mellanby's face grew grave again. 'I don't think we'd better risk it, Sally. We don't know how soon the workmen may descend on the place – and it's still very much our worry.'

'I do so *loathe* the idea. It was bad enough last night ...'

'I know ... But it's safer, Sally, really – I'm sure we must go through with it. Once we've finished the job, we'll be out of danger whether your theory turns out to be right or wrong ... You won't have to do very much – I'll be able to manage most of it myself ...'

'I hate it for you, too,' Sally said. She looked very downcast, 'Still, if you're quite certain ... What shall I tell Kira?'

'I should say we're going to see how that "dig" at Bensworth is getting on – she knows we've been there several times before so she won't be surprised. Then, just before dark, we can telephone her and say the car's broken down – we didn't have to use that story last night, so it's still all right. We can tell her not to wait up for us. I'm sure everything will go quite smoothly.'

'That sounds like famous last words ...! I feel horribly scared.'

'There's no need to be,' Mellanby said. 'By this time tomorrow, with anything like luck, it'll all be over ... Just one more effort, Sally!'

She gave a dejected nod, and turned away.

Chapter Thirty-One

It took Mellanby only a very short time to discover from the two motoring organizations he belonged to that neither of them had issued foreign touring documents for the Sherstons' caravan or car in the past week or two. It was just possible, he realized, that Sherston had sold them or stored them somewhere and gone abroad without them, but unless he'd had some special cause for alarm it seemed unlikely. The odds were great that he was still in the country – and Mellanby now faced the more complicated problem of finding him. First, he put in another call to the organization with the more extensive network of road patrols.

'That caravan I was asking you about just now,' he said, 'XAT 0391 . . . It seems it hasn't gone abroad, so it must still be around somewhere – touring, I imagine . . . Is there any chance you could help me to trace it, do you think? It's a matter of the greatest urgency.'

The official at the other end was friendly. 'Is it a case of illness, sir? If it's a life-and-death matter you'd probably do better to get in touch with the BBC – they might put out an SOS for you.'

'No, it's not that sort of thing,' Mellanby said. 'It's a business matter. George Sherston, the owner of the caravan, is an associate of mine, and it's absolutely vital I get in touch with him right away . . . It's a question of a big foreign contract . . . Naturally, I'd pay all expenses. In fact, I'd be quite prepared to drop in a blank cheque at your Area Office . . .'

'Oh, I hardly think that would be necessary . . . Have you any idea what part of the country Mr. Sherston might be touring in?'

'That's just the trouble I haven't . . . He was here in the Bath district in August, and then he went off into the blue . . . He could be anywhere – Wales – Scotland . . .'

'Has he any relatives or friends who might be able to help, sir?'

'No, he comes from overseas – I don't know of anyone in this country.'

'I see . . . Well, what's the caravan like?'

'Oh, it's a big one – more than twenty feet long, I should think. I can't tell you the make, but it's quite a luxury job.'

'What colour is it, sir?'

'Cream.'

'M'm! – it's a popular colour . . . What about the car?'

'A black Chrysler saloon – very smart and new.'

'That sounds more hopeful . . .' There was a little pause. Then the official said. 'Well, Mr Mellanby, we'll do what we can for you . . . We shall have to get in touch with our Area Offices, and they'll have to pass the word through to the patrols. If your friend is using the main roads, one of our chaps is bound to pick him up before long . . . It may take a day or two, of course.'

'I realize that,' Mellanby said. 'I'm sure you'll do the best you can . . . Every hour counts.'

'We'll get on to it right away, sir – and the moment we hear anything we'll ring you.'

'I'm most grateful,' Mellanby said. 'I'll be standing by . . .' He hung up. After a moment he put in a call to the other organization.

Chapter Thirty-Two

The day was completely overshadowed by the macabre task ahead. Sally's announcement that she and Mellanby were going out again was received philosophically by Kira, but with laments from the children, who were beginning to feel slightly neglected. Sally, instead of soothing them, became irritable. After her sleepless night she felt quite worn out. The weather didn't help. The air was close, with a hint of thunder, and she had a nagging headache which aspirin had failed to cure. Probably, she thought, it was a protest against what she had to do. She tried not to dwell on the lonely quarry and the nerve-racking vigil in the lane that would last most of the night, but she couldn't command her thoughts. Now that the moment was so near, she found it almost impossible to believe that they were actually going to do what they'd planned. She had the deepest forebodings, far stronger than at any time before. The decision to look for the caravan, the hope of a dramatic new turn in the affair, had undermined her resolution. She scarcely knew, now, how she would face the night.

Mellanby's mood was more determined, but hardly less sombre. Worse even than the odious task itself was the thought that Sally must take part in it. In his anxiety to spare her all he could, he spent much of the morning trying to work out a method by which he could get the body out of the grave without her help. It would be too heavy for him to lift from the bottom of the hole without assistance, but he might be able to raise it by mechanical means. He had some tackle in the shed that he'd once used for lifting bits of masonry – a simple arrangement of blocks and ropes which would require only a support from above. There was a tree bough, he remembered, if he could reach it . . . He'd better take the short pair of steps – they would just go into the car boot . . . With the tackle, he should be able to raise the body and swing it out on to the tarpaulin. Then he could wrap it up and rope it . . . Sally would see nothing . . . But he'd still need her help to get it from the bushes to the field opposite and that would be gruesome enough . . .

For a moment he stood gazing with clouded eyes over the peaceful garden. It seemed impossible that they had really come to this – *they*, the Mellanbys, with their sheltered life. To dig up a putrefying corpse in the night . . .! But one thing had led to another, and now there was no escape . . . Better not to think about it – better to concentrate again on the practical things. They would need water for washing this time – soap, towels . . . The physical effects, at least, could be obliterated. What of the mental effects, though – the incalculable aftermath . . .? 'Not poppy nor mandragora . . .!' Yet it had to be done . . .

The afternoon dragged slowly by. Five o'clock came. In another thirty minutes they would be off. Mellanby felt thankful they'd arranged to leave early – it would be less of a strain, killing time on their own . . . Restlessly, he returned to the garage for a final check on the equipment. The air was more oppressive than ever. He went over the items, and drifted back into the house. He couldn't keep still. Sally was giving the children their tea. Her cheeks were a hectic pink – she'd made up her face to hide her pallor, and overdone it . . . She was saying something to Kira about Tony's pyjamas . . .

At that moment there was a vivid flash of lightning, and a roll of thunder that shook the house. Almost at once it began to rain. Mellanby went to the sitting-room window and looked anxiously out. The storm had come up with astonishing speed. The purple sky was full of menace. The rain was getting heavier every second – it was almost a tropical downpour now. In a short time the garden paths were running like rivers. Water cascaded down the front of the house from the overflowing gutters. As he gazed out on the drenched scene, Mellanby knew that, for this night, at least, they had worried unnecessarily.

Presently Sally came and joined him at the window. Her face wore such relief as Mellanby had never seen there. 'The best-laid schemes, darling . . .!'

He nodded grimly. 'We couldn't go now, even if it stopped right away – and it's obviously not going to . . . We'll just have to put it off till tomorrow.'

'Perhaps it's Providence,' Sally said.

Chapter Thirty-Three

The storm raged till late in the evening, and then slowly died away. By morning the weather was fine and sunny again, with a brisk touch of autumn in the air – but the ground was still so wet that Mellanby thought they'd probably have to wait another twenty-four hours or so before they could move the body. Immediately after breakfast he got out the Humber and drove over to the quarry to see what conditions were like there. The first thing that caught his eye as he turned into Blackett's Lane was a huge lorry, dumping a load of brick rubble on the verge for the foundations of the new road. The sight gave him a shock. The Highways Department were getting busy even sooner than he'd feared. From now on there'd be constant comings and goings by day – and before long there'd be roadside camps and night-watchmen's huts as well. If he and Sally were going to move Roscoe at all, they'd *have* to do it within the next day or two. Mellanby drove on anxiously to the quarry.

One glance was enough to tell him it would be hopeless to attempt anything that night. The bushes surrounding the grave were standing in a pool of water, like mangroves in a swamp. In places the pool was several inches deep. The field across the way looked drier on the surface, but the spongy soil proved to be saturated. A hole dug there would fill up straight away. Mellanby spared a moment to assure himself that the turf over the suitcase hole hadn't been disturbed by the torrential rain. Then, in a very worried frame of mind, he drove home to tell Sally the news.

As he braked in the drive he heard the telephone ring. He walked quickly into the house. Sally was taking the call in the sitting-room. She broke off as he entered, said, 'Here he is – he's just come in

'...' and handed the receiver over. It was one of the motoring organizations.

'Hallo, Mr Mellanby?' the friendly official said. 'Well, we've got a bit of news for you – we think we may have located the caravan ... Tell me, is your Mr Sherston a big man of about fifty, with a young, good-looking wife?'

'That's right'

'Then we *have* found him. He's not too far away from you, either – he's in the Forest of Dean, in Gloucestershire.'

Mellanby threw a swift glance at Sally. 'Why, that's fine ...! My word, you've been quick.'

'Oh, we had a real stroke of luck, sir ... It seems that one of our Gloucester chaps was actually stopped by Mr Sherston near Cinderford yesterday afternoon – your friend wanted to know the way to the Forestry Commission's camping site, and our man directed him. When he got back from patrol last night and read the message we'd sent out, he remembered the black Chrysler and the cream caravan and reported them. He wasn't sure of the registration number – that's why I asked you to confirm the description ... Anyway, there seems no doubt about it now – and I don't think you'll have any more difficulty. Your friend was obviously making for the site, so if you can get over there right away you should find him.'

'I'll do that,' Mellanby said. 'Where exactly is this place?'

'It's near Berry Hill, about a mile and a half north of Coleford on the way to Symond's Yat. There's only one official site in the Forest, so you can't make any mistake.'

'Good ...' Mellanby jotted down the directions.

'We'll keep our chaps alerted in the meantime, Mr Mellanby, just in case the caravan has left.'

That's very kind of you ... I really am most obliged for all you've done.'

'Not at all, sir. Always glad to help a member.'

'I'll let you know what happens ... Don't forget to send me your account.'

The official chuckled. 'We won't, sir. Goodbye.'

Mellanby hung up and turned to Sally, who'd been excitedly following the conversation beside him. 'Well, there we are! – it looks as though the showdown with Sherston is going to be sooner than we thought ... Come on, let's go to Gloucestershire ...!'

Chapter Thirty-Four

They were away in the Rover before eleven. Sally took the wheel. Mellanby, whose leg had been giving him a bit of trouble since the arduous digging operation at the quarry, sat beside her with the road map on his knee. Not that he needed to refer to it much. The route was very straight forward – Chipping Sodbury and Stroud, then through Gloucester, then ten miles to the south-west, and they'd be at the edge of the Forest. Fifty-odd miles in all – say an hour and a half, the way Sally was driving today. One good night's sleep had obviously done her a world of good. By comparison, with the previous day, she seemed almost cheerful.

Mellanby was beginning to feel a little better about things, too, for a great weight had been lifted from his mind. He had never expected that Sherston would be traceable so quickly – all his plans had been based on the opposite assumption. Now it looked as though they might be seeing him in a couple of hours. If so, he could be roped in to help with the digging, as Sally had wanted him to be in the first place. Whether or not her theory about him was true – and now that all element of flight had been removed Mellanby was even more dubious – at least she wouldn't have to substitute for him in the lane again. That nightmare, at any rate, was over . . .

They didn't talk very much on the journey. Sally, eager to reach the camp and get the showdown over, was concentrating hard on the traffic. Mellanby puffed reflectively at his pipe and mentally rehearsed his part in the coming interview. It *was* going to be difficult . . . Unless the man had some quite unforeseen explanation of his conduct it could hardly be friendly. A strange man, Sherston

... A man with quite a lot of rugged charm in his way, and yet
...

Sunk in his thoughts, Mellanby scarcely noticed their passage
through Gloucester – but once they were out on the Cinderford
road he began to sit up and take an interest. They had been through
the Forest two years ago with the children – Alison had been a
mere toddler, then – and he'd loved it. They'd finished up in the
Wye Valley, he remembered – a wonderful day ... Carefree ...!
He started to look around for familiar landmarks. Actually, this
eastern part of the Forest wasn't very attractive – there had been
a lot of coal-mining going on, as well as forestry, and though many
of the old slag heaps were clothed now with grass and bracken,
they hardly improved the landscape. Cinderford itself was like its
name – a drab little mining village. But farther on, the road became
very picturesque, with giant oaks and beeches lining the route, and
intriguing vistas down the plantation drives, and pigs and sheep
wandering at will over the highway ... Here, the Forest was just
as Mellanby remembered it – and just as lovely ... It was probably
looking its best today, he reflected, with its stands of green conifers
bright after the rain, and the leaves of the deciduous trees showing
their first tints of autumn. A heavenly place ... It could be so good,
he thought, simply to be alive ... Perhaps it would be again one
day!

They reached Coleford soon after twelve and quickly found the
minor road that led to Symond's Yat. Now tension had returned
to the car, for they were very near their destination. It wasn't
necessary to ask the way to the site – almost at once they caught
the gay sounds of people on holiday, and a moment later Mellanby
spotted the notice – NATIONAL FOREST PARK CAMPING
GROUND. Sally turned the car in through the wide oak gates and
continued along an asphalted drive. The site was a pleasant,
smooth-mown field with a fine view, sloping gently down to thick
woods. On the left there was a sign marking the warden's bungalow.
High on the hill there was some kind of pavilion. The field made
a colourful picture, with its caravans, tents and cars of every

description and hue. Children and dogs were darting about, radios were playing, women were preparing lunch, men were carrying water from the stand-pipes and emptying rubbish into the dustbins. Everyone seemed very busy and very cheerful . . . Sally drove slowly round the oval track, while Mellanby looked about him for the Sherstons' van. A great many of the caravans were cream-coloured – but the Chrysler, at least, should be conspicuous . . . They drove round twice. By then, Mellanby had examined every van and car – and he knew they'd had their journey for nothing. The Sherstons weren't there.

Sally looked very crestfallen. 'I suppose he changed his mind and didn't come after all . . . What a wretched anticlimax!'

'Perhaps he came, and left again,' Mellanby said. 'Let's go and ask at the bungalow.' They parked the car and walked up to the house.

The warden was friendly, and as helpful as was possible. The caravan *had* been there, he said – he remembered the Chrysler, and he had a record of the number. It had been parked below the pavilion, next door to the blue-and-white van they could see – but it had stayed only the one night. He had no idea where it had gone.

Mellanby thanked him, and they turned dejectedly away. They were back at the beginning again now – there seemed nothing to be done but telephone the motoring people and tell them the hunt was still on . . . Then Sally suggested they should have a word with the owner of the blue-and-white van, in case he knew anything, and they walked over to it. A bald, plump man in a pair of very tight shorts was playing Jokari with an equally plump youth on the grass outside the door. From the caravan came an appetizing smell and the sound of frying.

Mellanby waited till the ball had come to rest, and then addressed the man. 'I'm sorry to bother you,' he said, 'but we're looking for some friends of ours – a man and a woman with a cream caravan and a black Chrysler car. We understand they were here last night . . .'

'That's right' the man said, 'they were our neighbours. Very nice people . . . They left this morning.'

Mellanby nodded. 'They didn't happen to say where they were thinking of going next, did they?'

'As a matter of fact they did,' the man said. 'This site was a bit too lively for them – they said they were going to some place on the other side of Monmouth . . . Not a camp, I gathered – just a quiet spot someone had recommended to them . . .'

'Did they mention the name of the place?'

'I believe they did, but I'm dashed if I remember it now . . . Something "Wood," wasn't it Dennis?' The youth looked vague. 'A Welsh-sounding name . . . Just a minute, let me get my map . . .'

The man disappeared into the caravan. Mellanby and Sally eyed each other anxiously. In a moment he was out again with an ordnance survey map of the district which he opened out on the grass. For a few seconds he studied it Then his finger pounced. 'That's the place – Trefant Park Wood . . . I knew it sounded Welsh.'

Mellanby bent over the map. A few miles to the west of Monmouth, and seven or eight from where they were, a large area of green was shown. Trefant Park seemed to be the name of the whole area. He looked at Sally. 'Well, I suppose we'd better go there . . .'

'I'm sorry I can't be more definite,' the man said. 'It'll be a bit like looking for a needle in a haystack, I'm afraid . . . Still you might find him.'

'We'll have a try, anyway,' Mellanby said. 'We're much obliged to you . . .' Sally smiled at the man, and with fresh hope they walked back to the car.

Chapter Thirty-Five

It was nearly one o'clock when they dropped steeply down into the little town of Monmouth. Mellanby managed to buy the inch-to-the-mile map of the district before the shops shut, and over lunch at a pleasant inn called the Crown they studied the terrain. The total area of Trefant Park Wood was nine or ten square miles. The ground was undulating, with a highest point of about four hundred feet. Not all of it was wooded – white patches on the map indicated open spaces in the interior. The place was completely girdled by a minor road, which seemed to be the obvious starting point for the search. From the road, at least a dozen tracks went off into the woods. The whole place appeared to be very sparsely inhabited. They were going to need, Mellanby thought, a lot of luck.

They quickly finished lunch, and by half past two they had reached Trefant Park and started their first circuit of the road. The wood turned out to be mainly an unfenced area, very like a continuation of the Forest of Dean but without plantations. While Sally drove, Mellanby inspected each entrance to it, peering through the openings in the trees for any sign of the van. The ground was so wet everywhere that it seemed unlikely Sherston would have risked getting bogged down off the beaten paths. That should help.

It took them an hour to make the circuit. Repeatedly they stopped, to inspect promising but half-concealed sites beside the road, or to seek information at the scattered cottages. By mid-afternoon they had still found no trace of the van. Then they began the more arduous part of the search – the combing of the interior. One by one, they explored the silent tracks that ran deep into the wood. Sometimes they were saved trouble by the absence of tyre marks in a soft surface. Sometimes they had to continue through a maze of drives for miles. Several times they got lost. It was a relief when, from time to time, they came upon patches of more open moorland country. Where the ground was undulating, it was possible to scan wide sweeps through the glasses, and save much time. There were places, though, that needed a closer look – a quick sortie on foot to inspect likely-looking spots, half-hidden by gorse or scrub, or cut off by the contours. It was at one of these, in the late afternoon when they had almost given up hope, that they found what they were looking for.

They had turned off the road along a firm, stony track that almost at once emerged from woodland into an open expanse of heather-dotted turf. According to the map, the track wound its way down to a shallow valley a quarter of a mile ahead, with a stream and more trees beyond. The valley wasn't immediately visible, because of a hump in the ground. Once over the hump, a beautifully secluded and picturesque spot was revealed – and there, beside the stream, were the cream caravan and the Chrysler.

Sally stopped the car. She looked as though she couldn't quite believe it. Mellanby, with a grunt of satisfaction, examined the caravan through his glasses.

'Can you see them?' Sally asked.

'Not a sign – but if the car's there, they must be.'

She reached for a cigarette, and lit it. 'How do you feel, darling?'

'Pretty keyed up . . .!'

'So do I . . . I wish they hadn't stopped in quite such an isolated place.'

'Why . . .? You're not expecting Sherston to get violent, are you?'

'I shouldn't think so – though if he did kill Roscoe . . .'

'*If* . . .! I'm sure there's nothing to worry about, Sally. We'll feel our way, and go easy on accusations to start with . . . If you do get a chance, take Eve off on her own and find out what she remembers. We'll decide the next step when we've compared notes . . . All right?'

'All right darling.'

'Then let's go!'

Chapter Thirty-Six

As Sally braked beside the Chrysler, the caravan door opened and Eve Sherston looked inquiringly out. For a moment she just stared at them, her expression as blank and unwelcoming as though they'd been complete strangers. Then she smiled. It was the familiar, fascinating smile – but this time you could almost hear it click on.

'Well, of all things . . .!' she exclaimed. She turned and called into the caravan. 'George, it's the Mellanbys!'

Sherston appeared in the doorway beside her. He, too, looked pretty blank. 'Why, hallo, you two . . . this *is* a surprise . . .!' His tone grew heartier. 'Nice to see you again – do come along in . . . Funny thing, we were saying only last night it was about time we rang you . . . How did you manage to find us?'

'It wasn't too difficult,' Mellanby said. 'We got the motoring people to help – and you left quite a good trail . . . How are you both?'

'We're fine, thanks – been enjoying a good rest haven't we, Eve? Needed it, too, after that business in Bath . . . Well, what about a drink to celebrate?' He reached tentatively for a bottle from the table. There was whisky and sherry, Mellanby saw, and four clean glasses set out on a tray.

'We're expecting some friends along later,' Sherston explained. 'Nice young couple we met in Gloucester the other day – but they won't be here yet . . . Will you have something, Sally?'

'No thank you,' Sally said. 'It's a bit early for me.'

'And for me,' Mellanby said.

'Sure? Oh, well . . .' Sherston looked hard at Mellanby, seeming suddenly to notice the seriousness of his manner. 'Nothing wrong, is there?'

'As a matter of fact,' Mellanby said, 'there is. Things have been going wrong ever since you left. That's why we're here.'

'Oh, lord! – bad news, eh . . .? In that case, I think perhaps *I'll* have a drink, if you don't mind . . .' Sherston poured himself a sizeable whisky, and drained it neat. After a moment he gave a wry grin. 'Right – now I'm fortified . . . What's the trouble, John?'

Sally looked at Eve. She was leaning forward with her arms on the table, listening intently. There was clearly no hope of detaching her at present.

Mellanby said slowly, 'Well – the first thing that happened was a letter from a man whom Roscoe had defrauded of seven thousand pounds.'

Sherston's jaw dropped. '*No . . .!*'

'We were pretty shaken ourselves,' Mellanby said.

'I'm not surprised . . . Do you mean the letter was to you?'

'No, it was to Roscoe. From a man named Faulkner. There'd been some correspondence between them and he knew the address.'

'What did the letter say?'

'It said Faulkner was going to put the police on to Roscoe. I knew we couldn't risk any inquiries. So I went to see Faulkner and paid him the seven thousand pounds to keep him quiet. I said I was doing it out of gratitude to Roscoe.'

'Good God! – that was pretty drastic . . . Wasn't there any other way?'

'*I* couldn't think of one.'

'*Well . . .!*' Sherston looked utterly taken aback. 'Why on earth didn't you get in touch with me right away?'

Mellanby shrugged. 'I had to move quickly – it was a question of hours.'

'I see . . . Well, I'll pay my share, of course, if you don't mind waiting a bit. I must say it seems a hell of a lot of money to throw away – but I can see your problem . . .'

'That wasn't the worst problem,' Mellanby said grimly. 'We learned a few days ago that the council are going to widen Blackett's Lane.

They're bound to break up the verges – and if Roscoe's body is still there when they do, they'll find it.'

There was a moment of absolute silence. Sherston sat very still. Eve's lovely complexion had turned blotchy.

Sally said, 'Eve, wouldn't you like to come out for a bit while they talk about it? It's so horrible . . .'

Eve shook her head. 'I want to hear . . . When are they going to start, John?'

'Almost any day now.'

'God, what a piece of lousy luck!' Sherston said. 'Who'd ever have thought of a thing like that . . .? A narrow bloody lane that leads nowhere . . .!' He broke off, his face dark. 'Well, we'll have to get to work again, that's all – move the body to a new place . . .'

'Sally and I have already been at work,' Mellanby said quietly.

'*What?*' There was a sharper note in Sherston's voice now – sharper and more apprehensive than the situation seemed to warrant, unless he had some secret sense of guilt about the body in the grave.

'Sally and I have already moved the suitcase,' Mellanby said. 'We'd no idea it would be so easy to find you – we thought we'd better go ahead on our own . . . It was quite a job – we spent the greater part of a night out there . . .'

Sherston had quickly recovered his poise. 'Hell, I really am sorry about this, John – you and Sally have been carrying the whole thing on your shoulders . . . Anyway, *I'll* take care of the body – you needn't worry about it any more . . . I can easily manage it on my own.'

Mellanby felt almost sure now. With a glance at Sally, he moved in to the assault. 'You certainly dig much faster than I do,' he said.

There was a moment of silence. Then Sherston said, 'I should – I'm a good bit stronger . . .'

'Even so, I've been wondering how you managed to dig Roscoe's grave in less than an hour and a half.'

'I just kept sweating at it, old chap.'

Mellanby shook his head. 'I don't think that was it . . . In fact, I *know* you couldn't have done it in the time.'

Sherston ran his tongue over his dry lips. 'What the hell are you suggesting?'

'I'm not suggesting anything – yet. I'm merely asking you for an explanation.'

'There's nothing to explain. You're wrong – that's all.'

'I'm quite sure I'm not wrong. It's something I happen to know about.'

Sherston shot a glance at Eve, avoiding Mellanby's eye. He said nothing.

'Of course,' Mellanby went on, 'One explanation could be that Roscoe was in a much worse state than I thought. Perhaps you *knew* he was going to die, and dug the grave in readiness?'

'Good God, you don't imagine . . .?'

'No – on the whole I don't think I do. There could be another explanation. Perhaps you killed him because you hated him.'

'You must be out of your mind . . .!'

'Well,' Mellanby said, 'it's something we shall have no difficulty in checking up on when we move the body. When *we* move it, Sherston – you and I. If by any chance you did kill him, there'll almost certainly be marks.'

Very slowly, the look of outraged anger faded from Sherston's face, giving place to deep anxiety. From Eve in the corner came a breathless 'Oh, God . . .!' as she covered her face with her hands.

The silence was broken by the clink of glass. Sherston was reaching for the whisky bottle, pouring himself another tot. 'Well, John,' he said, 'you've got me against the ropes, so it looks as though I'll have to tell you the truth.'

Mellanby waited. He hated the role of inquisitor.

'I've been afraid this might happen, ever since the night . . . I thought you'd probably realize there hadn't been time for the digging . . . You're quite right, of course. I *did* kill him.'

There was a little gasp of horror from Sally. Eve, wild-eyed, looked up. 'He didn't mean to, Sally I *knew* he didn't . . .'

'No,' Sherston said, 'I didn't mean to. It's true I hated him –

more than anyone I've ever met – but I'd never have done that . . .
You've got to believe me, John.'

'What happened?'

Sherston took a long breath. 'It was just after midnight Eve had
taken her tablets and was asleep on the bed over there – dead to
the world. I was sitting out here, and Roscoe was on the bed in
the end room – only half-conscious, I thought. Then, suddenly,
there was a noise, and I looked up, and he was coming out, crazy-eyed
and lurching a bit, with his hands raised in front of him . . . I could
see he was going to attack me. I'd put the spanner down somewhere
and I couldn't find it. There was only one thing to do – I got up
and went for him with my fists . . .'

He broke off. His face was shining with sweat and he mopped
it a little. 'Honestly, all I meant to do was stop him.'

'Go on,' Mellanby said.

'Well, he caught hold of me, and we struggled. He wasn't as
strong as he had been, but he was still strong. I managed to get
him back into the end room and we fell on his bunk together. He
was like a wild animal – I knew he'd kill me if he got the chance
. . . I was fighting for my life, John. When I suddenly felt my hands
at his throat I gave him all I had . . . The next thing I knew, he'd
sagged back, and I saw that he was dead. And that's the whole
truth. I killed him – but I swear to God I never intended him to
die. I was simply defending myself.'

'Why didn't you tell me?' Mellanby said.

'I wanted to – but I didn't know whether you'd believe me or
not. It couldn't have looked worse. You knew I loathed his guts –
I'd said over and over again that he wasn't fit to live . . . It was I
who'd suggested he should be brought along to the caravan . . . I
was sure you'd think I'd meant to kill him all the time. There were
great purple bruises on his throat – it didn't *look* as though we'd
had a fight . . . Who was to say I hadn't attacked him in bed? Eve
was still sleeping it off, she hadn't stirred – so I hadn't even got
her as a witness. I didn't dare let you see him – I couldn't take the
risk. I thought if I could get him underground and say I'd buried

him for your sake as well as mine, I might just get away with it. So I dug the grave – and when I'd finished I rang you.'

'And let me think *I'd* killed him,' Mellanby said, in a flat voice.

Sherston gave a shamefaced nod. 'It was a lousy trick, I know . . .'

'It was unspeakable,' Sally said with passion. 'How *could* you?'

'The way I saw it I had no option. When you're in a real jam you think about yourself first of all . . . Anyway, there it is – the whole squalid truth. Now it's up to you. If you give me away, I'm finished, of course . . . Nobody will believe now that I didn't do it on purpose. It'll mean jail for life.'

Mellanby passed a weary hand over his face. 'What about Eve? You told her about it, I suppose? She was a party to the – trick?'

'Yes,' Eve said, 'I knew . . . George woke me and told me what had happened, after – after Roscoe was dead. He told me what he was going to do, and I agreed. I take all my share of the blame. I was frightened. *I* didn't think you'd believe him, either, John. I'm sorry . . . I know how you must have worried . . .'

Mellanby got slowly to his feet. 'Well – there doesn't seem to be anything more to say, does there?'

'What are you going to do?' Sherston asked.

'I don't know – you'll have to give me time . . .'

'Is it worth my while to move the body?'

Mellanby shrugged. 'Please yourself . . .!'

'I'll take a chance on you, then – I'll do it tonight.'

'You can't, tonight . . . The place is under water.'

'Then tomorrow night . . . You can forget about it, anyway – it's my responsibility now. I'll take care of everything . . . I don't expect you to forgive me, John, but I can't really believe you'll sacrifice Eve and me on account of Roscoe . . . Anyway, I'll give you a ring when the job's done, and hear the verdict. Okay?'

Mellanby gave a barely perceptible nod. 'Let's go, Sally,' he said.

Chapter Thirty-Seven

They drove away up the slope in a brooding silence. Sally's feelings were so mixed that she found it difficult to sort them out. She was both appalled and relieved. The truth had been very different from what she'd imagined – better in some ways, much worse in others. The thing that had shaken her almost more than Sherston's admission of the killing was the discovery of Eve's part in it all. It was a shock to find her so heartless ... Mellanby was having other thoughts. His face was set in a deep, puzzled frown. It wasn't until they reached the high road and turned for home that the silence was broken. Then Sally said, 'What are you thinking, darling?'

'That it's been a ghastly business – and still is,' Mellanby said.

Sally nodded. 'I suppose it could have been worse, though ... It *could* have been murder ... And at least everything's explained now.'

'We've only got Sherston's word for what happened.'

'Don't you think he was speaking the truth?'

'How can one tell?'

'Well, darling,' Sally said, after a moment, 'whether he killed Roscoe accidentally or on purpose, he did kill him – *you* didn't. You've nothing to blame yourself for any more – that's the main thing.'

Mellanby grunted. Presently he said, 'Would a semi-conscious man really become dangerous again so quickly?'

'I suppose he might.'

'Wouldn't he show some sign? Sherston was only a few feet away from him – a change of breathing would have been enough ... I'd have thought he'd have been more prepared ... And could *anyone* sleep through a fight in a caravan? The din must have been terrific – you only have to step into the place to start it shaking . . .'

Sally said, 'Yes,' unhappily, and Mellanby fell silent again. Perhaps, he thought, it would be better not to try to discuss it any more at the moment – or make any decisions, either. After a night's sleep, things might seem clearer . . . He took out his pipe and began to fill it, using the last few shreds in his pouch.

'Can we stop in Monmouth and get some tobacco?' he said. 'I'm right out.'

'Of course . . .' They were already entering the outskirts of the town and Sally began to look out for a shop. Most of them seemed to be shut. 'It must be early closing day,' she said.

'Oh, well, never mind . . . I'll probably be able to get some in Gloucester.'

They continued through the town and crossed the river. As they approached the station Mellanby suddenly said, 'There's one open,' and pointed to a little general shop with a tobacconist's licence. Sally looked around for a place to stop. A train had just come in, and there were a lot of people and cars about on the narrow road. The station yard seemed the best place. She pulled in, and they walked back to the shop together and made the purchase.

As they approached the car again, Mellanby noticed a man strolling along near the kerb with a bundle of papers under his arm – a neatly-dressed, elderly man with white hair. Mellanby couldn't see his face, but there was something vaguely familiar about him . . . In an unhurried way the man turned – and their eyes met . . . Mellanby gave a gasp of astonishment. Of all people in the world, it was Charles Faulkner!

The old man looked even more startled than Mellanby. For a moment he stood stock still. Then a smile of pleasure spread over his face and he advanced with hand extended. 'Mr Mellanby! Well, you're the last person I expected to meet here.'

'Extraordinary!' Mellanby said, staring. Then he remembered that Sally didn't know the man. 'Sally, this is Charles Faulkner – I took that cheque to him, remember . . .? My wife, Mr Faulkner.'

Faulkner gave Sally an old-fashioned bow. 'A really remarkable coincidence,' he said. 'But there – the world's a small place. I once ran into an old friend on the quayside at Bangkok whom I hadn't seen for twenty years ... Well, how are you, Mellanby? No further trouble over that scoundrel Roscoe, I hope.'

'No,' Mellanby said.

'I'm glad to hear that ... I still think your husband's action was quixotic, Mrs Mellanby, but I must admit his generosity has made a great difference to me.' Faulkner's shrewd eyes dwelt on Mellanby for a moment. 'Do you often come to these parts?'

'Very rarely – we've been visiting some people we know ... What are *you* doing, Mr Faulkner – holiday-making?' Mellanby was looking at the papers under Faulkner's arm.

'That's right,' Faulkner said, 'just for a few days ... I've always been fond of the Forest of Dean – especially at this time of year.'

'It's certainly very fine,' Mellanby agreed. 'You're staying here in Monmouth, are you?'

For a fraction of a second, Faulkner seemed to hesitate. 'Yes,' he said.

'At the Crown? It's a nice inn – we had an excellent lunch there today ...'

'No ...' Again there was that trace of hesitation. 'I'm at the King's Arms – it's also very good ...' Faulkner smiled benignly at Sally through the upper lenses of his glasses. 'Are you spending the night at the Crown? – if so, perhaps you'd care to join me in a glass of something after dinner?'

'That's very kind of you,' Sally said, 'but we're actually on our way home now ... Children, you know ...'

'Ah, yes ...' Faulkner glanced at the car. 'Well, in that case I mustn't detain you ... It's been very pleasant to meet you again, Mellanby. I shall always be grateful to you. Goodbye, Mrs Mellanby.' He smiled again, and raised his hat, and walked slowly away with short, prim steps.

'What a sweet old boy!' Sally said, as they got back into the car.

'Yes,' Mellanby said, in a preoccupied tone. He was watching the retreating figure. As Sally turned the Rover in the direction of Gloucester, he swivelled round and continued to look through the rear window. Faulkner had stopped walking, and was gazing after them. Then there was a sharp bend in the road, and Mellanby lost sight of him.

'Well – extraordinary isn't the word for it,' he said.

'It's the kind of thing that's always happening, darling . . .'

'Oh, I know one often meets acquaintances in the oddest places, but . . .' He broke off, frowning. '*I'd* have said he'd just come off that train.'

'What on earth makes you say that?'

'Why, the papers he had under his arm – a *Times,* a *Spectator,* and *Punch.* Just the thing for a five-hour journey from London – but an odd collection to carry about otherwise.'

'*Was* it the London train?'

'I don't know,' Mellanby said.

He relapsed into silence again. The car sped on. They had covered several miles when Mellanby suddenly said, 'Do you mind stopping again, Sally – at a telephone box?'

'Darling, you're behaving very strangely . . . What's the matter?'

'I'd just like to make sure about something . . .'

They went on for another mile. Then Sally braked. 'Well, there's your box . . . Do you want any change?'

'No, thanks . . . I won't be long.'

Sally watched him enter the box, look up a number, and dial. She saw him talking. His face looked strained. He talked for only a moment or two. Then he came quickly back to the car.

'Well?' she said.

'Faulkner *isn't* staying at the King's Arms – they don't know him there . . . I *thought* he hesitated.'

Sally stared at him. 'But that's fantastic . . . Why should he say he was?'

'He had to say something, because I pressed him . . . Sally, I'll swear he'd just come off that train. *I* believe he was waiting for someone to pick him up.'

'But wouldn't he have said so? He didn't *have* to tell us he was staying.'

'He might not have wanted us to know he'd come down for some special purpose ... Sally, I don't believe meeting him there *was* just a coincidence. Think of it! We come here because we want to talk to the Sherstons about Roscoe, and we meet a man I've only seen once before in my life, who's connected with Roscoe almost as much as we are. It's almost incredible that that could be just by chance ... *And* he told us a phony story ... Sally, perhaps he's here to talk about Roscoe, too!'

Sally shivered. 'Darling, you're being awfully sinister ... What exactly are you driving at? Do you mean there may be some connection between Faulkner and the Sherstons?'

'Perhaps.'

'How could there be? I don't understand at all.'

'Neither do I,' Mellanby said. 'All I know is that I'm not satisfied – not with anything. If you ask me, there's something very very odd going on. I may be wrong – but I've got to make sure ... Sally, let's go back to the caravan.'

Chapter Thirty-Eight

Twenty minutes later they were back on the slope overlooking the camp. They had been away from it for a little over an hour. At Mellanby's suggestion, Sally stopped the Rover at a point where it was still hidden from below by the curve of the hill, and they went cautiously forward on foot till they could see over the brow.

'Look – there's another car.' Sally said.

Once again, Mellanby studied the camp through his glasses. The second car, parked beside the Chrysler, was a smart Riley saloon. The caravan door was open, but the van itself appeared to be empty.

'I believe they're sitting out on the other side of it,' Mellanby said. 'I can see someone's foot . . .'

'Their guests must have arrived, darling – the young couple . . . Faulkner wouldn't have a car here, not if he came by train.'

'That's true . . .' Mellanby looked a bit deflated. 'Still, we may as well make sure now we're here.'

'Won't we have to have some reason for coming back?'

Mellanby thought for a moment. Then he took his gold watch from his wrist and slipped it into his pocket. 'I lost my watch somewhere,' he said. 'The strap broke . . . That'll do.'

They walked back to the Rover and got in. Mellanby said, 'I should let her run down in neutral – it'll be quieter . . .' Sally took the brake off and the car slowly gathered speed, trickling silently down the grassy track and coming to rest almost exactly opposite the Riley. Mellanby got out quickly, and together they walked round to the other side of the caravan.

A rug was spread on the grass in the yellowing evening sun,

with bottles on a tray beside it. There were four people there – the Sherstons, and two men. All four were on their feet, as though they'd sprung up in alarm at the sound of the Rover door. One of the men was Charles Faulkner.

But it wasn't on him that the gaze of Mellanby and Sally fixed itself in sudden, spine-chilling horror – it was on the other man.

For the other man was Frank Roscoe!

Chapter Thirty-Nine

It was a shattering moment. Sally gave a cry and clutched at the side of the caravan for support. Mellanby stood as though rooted, his face stiff with horror and disbelief. It wasn't possible – it *couldn't* be . . . He'd actually *seen* Roscoe dead in the grave . . .

For a second or two, no word of any kind disturbed the tableau. Faulkner had taken off his glasses and was quietly polishing them. Sherston and Eve looked almost childishly self-conscious. Roscoe was staring at Mellanby. It was he turning on the others with the authority of leadership, who harshly broke the silence. 'You damned fools! – I thought you said they'd gone home!'

Faulkner gave a faint shrug. 'I watched them drive off. How could I know they would come back?'

'I guess we've had it, Frank,' Sherston said.

Sally sat down on a hummock of grass, holding her head in her hands.

Mellanby looked round him in a dazed way. He could still scarcely believe it – yet this big man, with the remembered voice and the trace of a scar still on his cheek, was undoubtedly Roscoe, in the flesh and formidably alive. He could never have been in the grave. He hadn't died. As well as shock, Mellanby was feeling something else now. The final lifting of a giant weight. *Roscoe was alive!* The long, hideous nightmare was over. No more digging, no more racking anxiety, no more self-questioning . . . But still incredulity lingered. *How . . .?*

Roscoe said, in a mocking tone, 'Maybe you'd like to pinch me!'

A deep, consuming anger took possession of Mellanby. It had been a plot, of course . . . He could see it all, now – the pattern of it, anyway . . . The whole thing had been a diabolical conspiracy between these four from the beginning. The golden opportunity, the careful reconnaissance at his home, the 'accidental' encounter with the caravan . . . Roscoe's wolf act, the deliberate unpleasantness, the intolerable provocations – all leading up to the staged fight . . . The planned removal of the 'unconscious' man, the phony 'death', the hasty 'burial' . . . The well-timed letter from Faulkner, leaving Mellanby no option but to settle Sherston's bogus confession when exposure loomed, his eagerness to move the non-existent body on his own . . . Cunning, resourceful, utterly unscrupulous . . .

'You – *devils!*' Mellanby said softly.

'Oh, come,' Sherston protested. 'We're not as bad as that. Nobody's been really hurt, after all – and nobody's going to be. You don't have to have any anxiety on that score, Mellanby, even though you have found us out – we're not violent types. Only in fun – eh, Frank?'

Only in fun,' Roscoe said, with an uneasy smirk. 'A few well-rehearsed punches and a self-inflicted scratch or so . . .!'

Mellanby gazed incredulously round the circle of faces. The impassive old man . . . Eve, with her lovely smile and heart of ice . . . Sherston, looking as though he'd been caught in some minor schoolboy prank . . .

'Doesn't agony of mind mean anything to any of you?' he burst out 'Don't you realize what we've been through . . .?'

Oh, you're too soft Mellanby,' Roscoe said. 'You fret too much. You should learn to take things in your stride.'

'It was monstrous,' Mellanby said. 'The most monstrously wicked thing I ever heard of. If there's such a thing as retribution . . .!' He broke off, and dropped down beside Sally. 'Darling – are you all right?'

She raised her head and nodded. The colour was beginning to creep back into her cheeks. 'I'm better now . . .'

'Can I get you some water?'

'No, I'm all right . . . John, can't we go?'

'We will very soon,' he said. He got up and faced them again.

He had himself more under control now. 'How did you do it Sherston? How did you manage it? I *saw* you cover him up . . .'

Sherston gave a feeble grin. 'Not him, Mellanby. It was a window-dresser's dummy – one of our few props, sacrificed for the good of the cause . . . Four feet down, with a scratch mark on the cheek – it would have deceived anyone in the poor light . . . Quite well executed, don't you think?'

'Oh, yes, a most polished performance!' Mellanby said. '*All* of it.'

'Thank you . . .! I'm glad you're beginning to take it a bit more calmly . . .? We had bad luck, of course – if it hadn't been for that road widening nonsense, we'd have got clean away with it. I quite thought we had.'

'You were running some pretty big risks, weren't you?'

Mellanby said. 'Suppose I'd insisted on going to the police when I first saw the grave . . .?'

'What? – and invite a five-year jail sentence. . .? It wasn't very likely, was it? – not after the first shock . . . No one ever has!'

'You mean you've worked this before?'

Sherston's grin broadened. 'Well there *are* one or two other chaps around who firmly believe they killed Roscoe in a fight – aren't there, Frank?'

'There are,' Roscoe said. He had lit a cigarette and was beginning to look more at ease. 'You're not the only sucker in the world, Mellanby. One born every minute, you know! Not all suitable material for this particular routine, of course – but then we've got other lines . . .'

'It seems a very tortuous way of making seven thousand, pounds,' Mellanby said.

'Do you know a better one? It came off, didn't it? – or would have done if it hadn't been for that damned road of yours . . . That's the acid test – does it work? And seven thousand pounds in a month is hardly to be sneezed at – all tax free, don't forget . . .! *Is* it, Charles?' Roscoe's hand dropped heavily on Faulkner's shoulder. 'This is the real rascal, Mellanby. Never sailed under a flag in his life, of course, unless it was the Jolly Roger – but looks so much the part, don't you think? Can't you just see him at the Captain's table? A great actor . . . But then we're all quite proficient wouldn't you say?'

'Oh, you're proficient, all right,' Mellanby said. He was realizing more and more the consummate skill that had gone into the plot – the brilliant foresight . . . Roscoe giving precise details of his Army career, because he *wanted* to be exposed as a fraud . . . Roscoe making himself out to be footloose and friendless, so that when the time came his disposal would seem safe . . . The delicately poised Jekyll-and-Hyde act, to make sure he wasn't thrown out too soon . . . Eve's build-up of the jealous husband . . . Sherston's roughness and toughness . . . Faulkner's reluctance over the cheque . . . They hadn't missed a thing.

'You're a fine, predatory gang!' Mellanby said.

'That's it,' Roscoe agreed. 'That's what we are. Opportunity-hunters on perpetual safari . . .! Merchant adventurers . . .! And you'd be surprised what a lot of opportunities there are, Mellanby. All you need to do is get to know the right people – and believe me, you don't have to have introductions. You just look around to see who you can do a good turn to – the world's full of rich people who need helping in some way . . . Rescuing your wife and kid was just a lucky break, of course – that kind of chance doesn't often happen. But if you keep your eyes open you can always find people who need a bit of a leg-up. You can put them in your debt and you move on from there. If they turn out to be foolish, easily-hoodwinked people, you use Plan I – that's the straightforward confidence stuff. If they're sensitive, complex characters with consciences, you try Plan II – that's the one we used on you.'

'You're very frank,' Mellanby said.

'Well, old man, considering what you know about us already there's not much point in being anything else, is there? It's what they call a fair cop . . .! Not that we're in any real danger, mind you – we've always got our bolt holes open. If you showed any signs of causing trouble we'd scatter at once. We'd be out of the country before the police had even got the particulars down. But

I'm sure that's not going to arise – you're not going to give us away.'

'What makes you think that?'

'My dear fellow, what would you gain by it? It's the same question you had to ask yourself when you thought you'd bumped me off – and the answer's the same. Absolutely nothing! Not even the satisfaction of getting your own back on us, because as I say we wouldn't be here ... Of course, if we did happen to muff the get-away we'd be jailed for years – but then we'll probably be jailed in the end, anyway. It's an occupational risk, we know that ... Why should you ruin yourself trying to hurry things up?'

'Ruin myself?' Mellanby looked startled.

'Well, wouldn't you? Aren't you a respected figure in Bath – prominent on committees, looked up to by everyone, wife with hosts of friends, growing children socially welcomed – all that sort of thing ...? What do you think would happen if you told your story in court? Maybe you haven't thought what it would sound like?'

'As a matter of fact I haven't,' Mellanby said.

'Then, you'd better think fast, chum. I can just see your evidence spread all over the local paper – how you thought you'd killed a man, a man who'd saved the lives of your wife and child, so you let your accomplice bury him secretly and told a lot of lies about how he'd gone away, and kept the facts from the police ... And how you planned to dig up the body when things got too hot for you ...! Oh, yes, all your friends are going to like that a lot – you'll look such a fine citizen, such a law-and-order man ...'

'I'll be able to explain everything,' Mellanby said uncertainly. 'The position I was in ... It's not as though I committed any crime.'

'A fat lot of good that'll do you! – you behaved as though you had. I tell you your name would stink. You'd be finished, Mellanby ... And for what?'

Mellanby mopped his damp forehead. 'I suppose it wouldn't sound very nice ...'

'*Nice!* – it would sound bloody awful ...! And that's not all – you'd be a laughing stock ... You've been a frightful sap, Mellanby, let's face it – and that's exactly what you'd look – a sap. Naïve and credulous. Believing everything you were told. Playing along with a bunch of crooks and not realizing it . . . And those pathetic attempts of yours to defend yourself – I'd take good care that all that came out you know. Getting knocked around your own sitting-room and not being able to raise a finger! Falling for a lot of melodramatic threats! Too scared even to get the police in! Why, the other kids would be calling after yours in the streets – "How's your sissy father?" You'd never have any respect from *them* again. They'd suffer, too. And all the other wives would be looking pityingly at your wife and thanking God *they* didn't marry a cowardly weakling like you . . .'

'*Stop!*' Sally was on her feet, her eyes blazing. 'It's not true what you're saying – any of it. He's not weak, and I'm proud of him, and so would anyone else be. He did everything he possibly could – *more* than he could. Didn't he try to stand up to you even though you're *you* that should be ashamed . . . *He* wasn't scared of going to the police – it was me. Everything he did was for me. God, how you've twisted things . . .!'

'I've put things the way your friends and neighbours will see them,' Roscoe said contemptuously. 'Do you imagine *they'll* go around making excuses for him? Not on your life! They'll crucify him . . . I tell you, Mellanby, if you don't keep your mouth shut you'll be changing your name and emigrating inside six months. On the evidence, there isn't a hope for you.'

Mellanby looked at Sally. 'I'm afraid he may be right, darling . . .'

'But, *John* . . .'

'After all,' Roscoe interrupted, 'this won't be the first time you've kept discreetly quiet for the sake of your family and your reputation, will it? You hushed things up when you thought you'd killed a man, which was a pretty big decision – it would be just plain bloody stupid to talk now . . . Of course, we wouldn't let you be the loser – you can have your seven thousand back. That goes without saying. You found us out so it's only fair . . . Anyway, we want to make things easy for you . . .' Roscoe looked around the watchful circle of conspirators. 'All right with you, George ...? Eve ...? Charles ...?'

There were nods from each of them in turn.

'That's settled, then ... We won't have made a penny out of the thing ourselves, Mellanby, and you won't have lost anything – so what is there for you to worry about ...? As a matter of fact, we'll be really generous ...' Roscoe stepped over to the caravan and took out a cheque book and wrote out a cheque against the wall. 'There you are – eight thousand pounds! A thousand extra for pain and suffering!'

Mellanby looked at the cheque. 'You think a thousand pounds covers what we've suffered!'

Roscoe grinned. 'I'd suffer a lot for that myself! It'll pay for a nice long cruise for the whole family, anyway – help you to get over things.'

'Will it be honoured?'

'It'll be honoured, all right. We've pulled off several lucrative deals lately, haven't we, George?'

'We have,' Sherston said. 'You needn't worry, Mellanby – it won't bounce.'

Mellanby hesitated. 'If I do take it, it won't mean I condone anything you've done ...'

'You don't have to,' Roscoe said. 'Take it, you damned fool – and thank your stars that's the end of the business.'

'Well ...' For a moment Mellanby still held back. Then, with a shrug, he took it. 'It is my own, after all ... And I don't see why I should wreck my life on account of a pack of scoundrels.'

'*John* ...!' Sally said, in a voice of anguish.

Mellanby looked at her stonily. 'Haven't we been through enough, Sally? – do we have to be pilloried as well ...? It's no good – I just can't stand any more trouble ... Come on, let's go home and try to forget all about it.'

He turned away before she could say any more, and started to walk towards the car. Sally followed, a dejected pace behind. The others went along, too. Mellanby dropped heavily into the driving seat. In silence, Sally took the seat beside him. The engine sprang to life. Mellanby stuck his head out of the window. 'You *will* all be jailed in the end, I'm sure of that . . . Someone will get you . . . And, by God, you'll have deserved it.'

He let in the clutch, and the car moved away up the slope. The last thing he saw in the driving mirror was Eve moving towards Roscoe, smiling. They were all smiling . . .

Chapter Forty

Sally was quiet till they reached the top of the bill. Then she suddenly exploded. 'John, *stop!* We've got to talk.'

With a readiness that surprised her, Mellanby swung the car off the track into the trees and turned the engine off. 'What is it?'

'John – we've got to tell the police.'

His face was expressionless. 'You think so?'

'We've *got* to, darling ... We were wrong to keep quiet before – I can see that now. I know it was all my fault, but we were *wrong* ... We can't do it again. We *mustn't!*'

'Are you sure?' Mellanby said. 'It couldn't have been made easier for us, you know ... It won't be like the last time – there's no danger any more, nothing to worry about. If we keep our own counsel now, nothing more can possibly happen. It really *is* all over ...'

'It's not all over, John – only for us ... You heard what they said – they'll do it again. They'll go on doing it. They'll make other people suffer, just as we did ... Darling, *someone's* got to stop them. Don't you see? – they're relying on people not telling – on everyone just thinking about themselves and taking the easy way ... You said yourself that if everyone did that, the world wouldn't be fit to live in – and you were right, darling, you were *so* right ... John, why do I have to say this? *Surely* you agree?'

Mellanby said quietly, 'Of course I agree.'

She stared at him. 'But – you talked as though you didn't ... You let them go on and on, persuading you ... You took the cheque as though it settled everything ...'

'I had to, Sally. If they'd had the slightest doubts about me, they'd have cleared off and got clean away . . . I had to make them feel absolutely sure and safe, so that they'd stay . . . That's all. I couldn't let you know, could I . . .?'

'*Oh* . . .' Tears suddenly glistened in her eyes – tears of relief. 'Oh, I'm so glad . . . I didn't realize. I couldn't understand what was happening to you – you seemed like a stranger . . . You were so terribly convincing.'

'Then with luck,' Mellanby said grimly, 'they *will* be there when the police come. I thought I was being rather ham myself . . .' His hand closed on Sally's. 'It's going to be pretty tough for us, Sally darling – you do know that?'

'Yes, I know . . . Will it be as bad as Roscoe said?'

'Well – somehow, I doubt it. Roscoe doesn't know much about decent people – they often don't behave the way you might expect . . . Do you remember reading about a boy who was court-martialled a few years ago because he sat down in a trench and wouldn't fight? He was a nice lad – he just couldn't take it. He went back to his village to face the contempt of his friends – and blow me if they didn't put the flags out for him all along the street . . .! You can never tell.'

'I don't think they'll put any flags out for us!'

'No, they won't — but they may not actually throw things . . .!' Mellanby gave a rueful smile. 'After all, there *are* worse things in the world than being a sap!' He leaned forward and switched on the engine. 'If I'm wrong – well, we'll just have to see it through, that's all.'

'Yes, darling,' Sally said. Her face was clear, her eyes untroubled. 'We'll see it through . . . Oh, John, isn't it wonderful to have absolutely nothing to worry about!'

www.ingramcontent.com/pod-product-compliance
Ingram Content Group UK Ltd.
Pitfield, Milton Keynes, MK11 3LW, UK
UKHW040105010325
455690UK00002B/12